Not a Hope in Hell

They said he was a trigger-happy sheriff, but when the bad boys came to town nobody complained when he cut loose with his guns.

Until the day when two elderly folk are killed during a shoot-out, forcing the sheriff to get out of town and find a new place to make a living. But when things don't work out as planned: the only place to go is back to Texas, where the wanted dodgers await, along with a whole crowd of other enemies. . . .

Not a Hope in Hell

Hank J. Kirby

A Black Horse Western

ROBERT HALE · LONDON

© Hank J. Kirby 2012
First published in Great Britain 2012

ISBN 978-0-7198-0544-8

Robert Hale Limited
Clerkenwell House
Clerkenwell Green
London EC1R 0HT

www.halebooks.com

Typeset by
Derek Doyle & Associates, Shaw Heath
Printed and bound in Great Britain by
CPI Antony Rowe, Chippenham and Eastbourne

PROLOGUE

SHOOT OR DIE

He didn't even know they were in town until Lars Andersen from the livery came panting into the law office by the back door, struggling to get breath enough to convey his message.

'Don't you go havin' a heart attck in my office, Lars!' Sheriff Clay Emory said, half-joking, though alarm bells were ringing in his head as he saw the state the livery man was in. A lanky, scrawny man, Lars, his pigeon chest was heaving with his efforts. Sweat ran down his flushed face as he waved his right arm, flapping the hand towards the front of the office.

'They here! In my stables. Jus' leave broncs that've been near ridden into – ground. Rough – bassards.'

'Who, Lars?'

Andersen swallowed audibly. 'The Bellmans. . . .'

Emory stood quickly behind his desk, all six feet plus one inch, and 185 pounds, taut as a blue-steel

5

spring. 'Heard Milo got killed in Laredo. This must be Jace and Banjo?'

He swore softly as Andersen nodded, getting some breath back now. 'They been ridin' hard – helluva hard. Mean as snakes, *Meaner*! Jace already belted my stable boy across the head for droppin' his saddle.'

By now Emory had drawn his six-gun and was checking the cylinder loads. Satisfied, he rammed it back into his holster and reached down a rifle from the rack. The heft of it told him it was fully loaded. He jacked a shell into the breech and a couple of long-legged strides took him to the street door.

'You go easy, Clay! They lookin' for trouble.'

'As always. Go back to your livery and keep your head down, Lar. See which way they went?'

'McQueen's. You want I should get a few men?'

Opening the door, Emory shook his head; he was being paid to wear the badge – only right he did the job that was needed.

McQueen's was the biggest of the two saloons in Fremont and ran the best whores. It was a good bet the Bellmans were aiming to kick over the traces – if not a whore or two – before moving on. Sounded as if they had already been drinking. Either way, their mood seemed dangerous and he knew it would come down to gunplay.

Emory didn't think of himself as brave, nor as fool-hardy. He had toted a badge on and off for five or six years when it was required, and had a string of tamed-down towns behind him where he was welcome at any time. He had added to the population of the boot hills of those towns; he'd brought Fremont into line in a bareknuckle way, too.

He was the kind of lawman they liked in that part of southern Texas, where all the badmen seem to gather so they could quickly slip across the Rio when the law started breathing down their necks too hard.

But this was going to be different: Clay Emory could see that as soon as he started across the street.

The Bellmans were already on the saloon veranda, guns drawn, waiting for him.

So that's how it was going to be! They'd been sent to nail him, probably. He knew he had trodden on the toes of some of the men who liked to think they ran this town – and various illegal operations across the Rio. He'd heard a whisper that there was a price on his head; too much law and order didn't suit everyone. Some said he was too damn quick on the trigger, but it was OK if stopping drunks and troublemakers needed a bit of gunplay: double standards.

There was no talking; the Bellmans didn't waste breath that way. Dark-skinned men with gunbarrel eyes, they preferred to let their guns speak for them.

People were running to get off the street now and Emory stopped just past midline and fired his rifle from the hip. It was a hurried shot, only meant to point the way this was going to go. No palaver: just shoot or die.

Which suited the Bellmans fine.

They separated, guns blurring into position with the speed they were famous – *infamous* – for.

The sheriff dived for the gutter, levering another

cartridge into the breech even as he rolled towards the edge of the saloon veranda. The Bellmans had fired together, far enough apart to make an intersecting angle, so that Emory would be caught in the crossfire.

Bullets kicked dust and grit inches from the lawman as he thrust up to his knees, startling the Bellmans by appearing so close, shooting as he rose above the level of the veranda. Jace grunted, bullet-slammed back against the wall, jaw dropping. Banjo looked startled; the Bellmans weren't used to anyone shooting back at them. Usually their first shots ended any confrontation, pronto.

Banjo stared at the blood on Jace's narrow face and fanned his gun hammer, barrel angled down towards the now crouching Emory. The sheriff's hat spun into the street and his head jerked as hot lead burned a furrow across his left cheek. It threw off his aim but, as he staggered, he worked the lever again and finished off Jace. The gunfighter's legs wobbled as he clawed at his chest with both hands, having dropped his gun. He pitched forward on to his face. His nose squishing against the floorboards brought a wolflike howl from Banjo and he tossed his empty gun at Emory, dived for his brother's fallen Colt.

Emory jammed the next cartridge, levering too fast, tossed his rifle aside as Banjo vaulted off the end of the saloon veranda. Like a wild man, he fired under his left arm as he dodged past the hitchrail and ran out into the street where a buckboard with a man and woman in the seat rocked and clattered as the team panicked; hot lead had been flying all over that section of the street. Banjo waved the six-gun wildly, causing the horses to veer suddenly. The grey-haired man lurched up in the driving seat, fighting the jerking reins, even as Clay Emory dropped to one knee, six-gun thundering.

Two bullets caught Banjo running, one in the back as the first took him low in the side and twisted him. The lawman fired again and yelled as the buckboard team reared and skidded, crashed into the dying outlaw in a flail of hoofs and blood-soaked clothing.

Banjo Bellman went down under the striking hoofs and the team staggered. The woman screamed as the buckboard reared into the air, hurling both passengers out of their seats, and crashed over, splintering and bouncing a couple of times before skidding to a halt. The harness had snapped and the now terrified team lunged to their feet and bolted down Main in full panic, trailing reins and splintered timber.

Sheriff Clay Emory froze in his tracks. He didn't even bother looking at Banjo – he knew he had to be dead.

What caught his attention, were the bloodied bodies of the elderly couple who had been riding in the shattered buckboard.

He jerked his head up as the door of the general store burst open and a young woman in a checked dress, her matching bonnet now askew in her hurry, came running towards the buckboard's wreckage.

She stopped, the back of a hand muffling her gasp as she looked at the still, bloodied couple. Then she turned a marble-white face towards Emory, who was automatically reloading his Colt.

He was not prepared for her hurtling body striking at him, knocking him off balance. Small, hard fists punched at his face. He dropped his gun, tried to cover up as her nails ripped at one eyebrow, grabbed her slim wrists.

'The hell're you doing?' Then he saw her face close up, recognized rising hysterics. 'Easy! *Easy*, miss!'

'You damn trigger-happy . . . killer!' she gasped, a little spittle flying, her body twisting and struggling to break his grip. Then she screamed, '*Murderer!*'

CHAPTER 1

A DEBT TO PAY

The Mexican guide was a lousy cook, but this particular batch of *frijoles* was the worst Clay Emory had ever tasted.

Sitting on the log, he poked his fork around the battered tin platter, turning over the mess. They looked normal enough, but. . . .

'How come you ain't having any beans, Miguel?'

The fat little Mexican with the hard eyes and drooping moustache smiled, shrugged his heavy shoulders. 'There not enough, *señor.*'

'Uh-huh. Well, I ain't all that hungry right now,' Clay lied. 'You can have some of these if you want.'

Miguel held out both pudgy hands, palms towards him. '*Aiyee, muchas gracias, señor,* but. . . .' He patted his ample waistline. 'My wife – she say I already too fat. That why she only pack small lot of *frijoles.* You have them, *señor.* I make do with *canapes.* You like one to mop up the beans?'

Emory shook his head. 'Think I'll pass.'

The small eyes pinched down to pinpoints but the

big teeth flashed in a stiff smile. 'I maybe put too much chilli in the *salsa*.' His grin widened as he said slyly, 'But the extra heat – she good for make the blood hot.' He shrugged and winked, nodded towards Emory's lower body. 'Keep the *señoritas* happy, eh?'

Clay frowned, not hearing the Mexican's words. His head was buzzing, his vision blurring. He lurched to his feet.

'You – son of – a bitch! You've – poisoned me!'

He groped for his six-gun but couldn't seem to control his hand, missing the holster and gun butt entirely. He felt his gorge rising and with a gurgling gasp flung himself towards some rocks, kneeling, stomach contracting – but not quite enough to eject its contents.

Vaguely wondering what the Mexican was doing, he rammed three fingers down his throat and made himself throw up. He was trying to straighten when something that felt like a boulder hit him on the back of the head and he fell forward, rolling to one side as his vision was suddenly shot through with lightning bolts and a whole mess of weird sounds and hisses rang in his ears.

Wherever he fell from, it was one hell of a long way down before he hit bottom.

Rock bottom, with an impact that jarred his brain loose in his skull.

The sun burned his eyeballs through the lids and he had enough sense to turn his head aside before he allowed his eyes to flicker open enough so he could see through small, blurred slits. He lay still for several minutes before opening his eyes fully, making sure the heat was on the back of his head. Even so, glare struck back at him from a pale rock and he screwed up his face again, moved his head away.

It caused him some pain as he rolled on to his side, stomach convulsing but producing nothing but a little bile.

He remembered the Mexican then, and the poisoned beans.

It took him almost twenty minutes to unknot his abused belly and locate his canteen, which was still attached to his saddle, to his surprise. He would have thought Miguel would have taken that – though maybe not. The son of a *puta* would've just taken the saddle-bags – with the money in them.

He managed to hold down a mouthful of water, allowed a little more to trickle over his burning tongue. He sat back against the sun-warmed boulder and rubbed his head. There was a raised weal on the left side, towards the rear, the skin split, caked with dried blood. *Gun butt*, he decided, and he was pleased with the bunch of epithets that spilled from his mouth, all directed at fat little Miguel – wherever the little bastard was!

The Mexican looked like a clown, harmless; but, well, a man deserved all he got for being so stupid as to put trust in appearances. Talk about playing the greenhorn!

He wasn't even sure where he was. The Rio should be to the north, maybe slightly west of north, but this was a part of Mexico he didn't know. Most of his border crossings had been more to the east, from around Laredo way.

What he should have done was spread a little of that money around the Mexican border guards and crossed in an area he knew. Wonderful thing, hindsight!

But a gringo, even one only suspected of gun-running, didn't have a hope in hell of surviving these days, not with the political situation being as it was in Mexico. Of course, there was always some kind of political upheaval down *mañana* way, but things were pretty sensitive right now: the gringos had a bad name because of the guns they were supplying to the *rebeldes* – strictly illegal.

There didn't have to be definite proof, just being a gringo was enough with some of these trigger-happy Mexes.

So he had played it safe – *safe*! Take a look around, you stupid, sick son of a bitch: this is *safe*? In country so barren some folk claimed this was where the moon had torn free of Earth and hurtled out into space, and you're standing here now, with no horse, no money. . . .

'And no goddamn redress!' he said aloud, flailing himself for being such a fool. Over thirty years old, with all that law-pushin' behind him, knowing what kind of men haunted this border country, and he had *trusted* his intuition, hired Miguel Delesandro on the say-so of a Durango whore who had the face of an angel.

'Hell, she'd likely drugged the damn tequila I was drinkin' at the time.'

Too late now. So what could he do? First, take stock Never mind what he didn't have, just concentrate on what he had and could put to some kind of use that would help him get out of here. That ought to be simple enough.

He had a saddle, but no horse to throw it on. So forget the horse for now! Half a canteen of water. He laughed briefly. That Miguel had a sense of humour; he had left a small bag of beans with the handful of coffee, neither of which Clay Emory would be game enough to eat or drink.

His six-gun was gone, a good Colt with a stag handle and a little fancy engraving on the barrel a friend had done for him long ago. There was still a rifle, but it wasn't his own Winchester. It was a battered old Henry that Miguel had carried. Although the Mexican had left a handful of semi-corroded rimfire ammuntiion with it, it was so old it would likely blow up in his face if he tried to shoot it!

What else? A blanket, also Miguel's, worn thread-bare, a handful of flour in a corner of an otherwise empty sack, some salt, and – hell! That was it!

He'd survived on less, but that was years ago and in country he knew a little about. Here, he might as well have been in the middle of Hell, looking for the Pearly Gates—

Just to punish himself a little more, he looked around at the shimmering land that had entrapped him: brown, grey, desolate, the teeth of broken crags snapping at the sky, stunted chaparral – miles and miles of it, not a splash of real green anywhere. Nor the flash of a waterhole.

He sighed and, favouring his sore belly, started gathering his things, shouldering the saddle optimistically, the ancient Henry rifle dangling from his right hand. Out of all the cartridges Miguel had left, he had found only six or seven he would trust to shoot – but only if he had to.

There was a good chance he would starve if he saw an animal and hesitated in case the rifle blew up in his face. *And if that happened, starving would hardly be an issue, would it, you dumb bastard!*

It didn't help to castigate himself: but he was damned if he could savvy how he had been so stupid! It wasn't like him. 'Marshal Caution' they had called him in one town, just north of Tombstone, but *that* wariness had been brought on by a near lynching he had decided to turn his back on, because the crime had been so horrific, a girl child victim and. . . .

They had been tossing the rope over a high branch of the umbrella-like cottonwood when he had been given irrefutable proof that the man about to swing was innocent.

By God! It had been a close-run thing! The man's eyes were bulging and his swollen tongue was filling his mouth as Clay had cut the rope.

That had slowed him down.

Even now he felt beads of sweat oozing out on his forehead, trickling down into the two-inch bullet gouge on his left cheek, before dripping from his clenched jaw.

Something like that would make anyone leery

about how he acted. Yet he had taken this damn Miguel at face value! After he had tossed down the tequila that beautiful whore had given him!

OK! You're looking for excuses, so say she had already spiked your drink and Miguel had likely been adding a little of whatever drug he had used in the food he had fed him along the trail, building it up in your body to a bigger dose, the last plate of *frijoles* finishing it off. Almost!

He felt nauseous and dizzy now; there was bound to be some residue still in his system, slowing him down, spinning his mind like a kid's whip-top. He dropped the gear, rummaged until he found the jar of salt, poured all of it into the tin coffee mug and filled it with water. His hands shook and he was sweating profusely as he stirred it into an opaque, semi-syrup and gulped it down, almost choking on its rawness.

But it did the job, almost turned him inside out, and if there was any residual drug or poison in his system after that then he was doomed and had to accept it.

Accept it or not, he was going to catch up with that damn Mex; this whole deal had started with him having a debt to pay, a big debt that had put him among the *pistola contrabandistas*. Now there was one more he had to square away.

In blood – and before he cashed in his chips.

Strictly speaking, it was not on the chief's agenda, but if Miguel led him where he expected to go, all would be well.

If not, he wouldn't care, because he'd be dead.

17

CHAPTER 2

DINERO

Miguel couldn't believe his luck.

'*Dios*!' he exclaimed as he pulled one of the canvas sacks out of the gringo's saddle-bags and saw that it was tied with a twist of wire: a wire with many twists, so it would take time to undo. But there was a quicker way.

Miguel used it; he took his belt knife with its honed blade and hacked into the tough canvas below the wired neck. *Ah!* He had known something was strange when he first removed the saddle-bags. He had heard the rustle of paper – *paper money!* – his ear was well attuned to the sound, but the bags were much too heavy for just paper currency.

Now he found out why; the curved blade sawed through the heavy canvas and into folded packs of greenbacks. But there had been a metal-to-metal sound, too, and he quickly used his stubby fingers to rip open the cut he had made. He glimpsed the packages of folding money and saw the yellow gleam inside the one his knife had damaged.

There was more than just paper currency here, much more. The bills had been used as wrapping, to stop the gold *pesos* from clinking.

'*Aiyeeee*!' he croaked, raising his eyes to the heat-pulsing sky. '*Gracias, Dio mio, muchas gracias!* You have made me rich beyond my wildest dreams!'

He hefted the other sacks, opened the second set of saddle-bags and found two more sacks with wired-up necks. His heart was hammering against his well-padded ribs. Sweat blinded him and he wiped it away irritably, flicking diamond-like globules from trembling fingers.

'Ah, gringo, I am sorry I poison you! You 'ave been mos' kind to old Miguel! You 'ave give me a life of ease and pleasure!' He laughed briefly. 'Ah, that *puta*! She bargain with me for fifty *pesos* when she find out you carry some *dinero*! But, she is too cheap! Mmmmm, very beautiful but – well, maybe I deliver her fifty *pesos* in person and make her give me something nice in return, eh?'

He sat back, mopping his face with a big kerchief, using one hand, the other fondling the gold coins and folded money in the first sack he had opened. *How much?* he wondered, and a figure came into his head out of nowhere.

'Maybe five thousand dollars! Five? No! Make it ten! Why not?'

Indeed, why not? He didn't know he had robbed

Clay Emory of more than $10,000, half of it in a mix of US and Mexican currency notes, the rest in gold and silver coins: *reales, Louis d'ors*, double eagles, high-value *pesos*. . . .

Any way you looked at it, Miguel Delesandro was a very rich man.

And, despite his comical looks, he was willing – and able – to fight to keep his bounty.

He was ready to kill anyone foolish enough to try to take it from him. Or was he?

The mistake he made was staying to gloat over his good fortune; in truth, he was stunned by the result of his little trick which he had played on several gringos, with the connivance of the angel-faced whore. Usually the drugged food netted him only a handful of *dinero*, and a horse that brought a few more dollars, all of which were too swiftly spent.

But this haul! *This haul* would last a long, long time. He would move south, he decided, to Mexico City. Set himself up in some kind of business. He smiled crookedly at the thought.

The kind of business where rich men would pay big money for the company of beautiful women!

He took a bottle of tequila from one of his own saddle-bags, uncorked it and drank deeply, easing his fat shoulders against a boulder, half-closing his eyes, allowing the dream to take over. . . .

Señor Miguel Delesandro – Don Miguel Delesandro! Aaah! Money could buy many titles.

He smiled, showing his crooked, yellowed teeth below the bushy moustache.

He died with that smile on his fat face, the bullet taking him squarely in the centre of the forehead.

The son of a bitch had lied to him! That was the thought that swirled into Clay Emory's throbbing head as he came over the broken ridge and saw the gleam of a river that could only be the Rio Grande. Wide but shallow here, the yellow paleness of sand showed through the greenish water.

It was only a few miles beyond the range of broken hills where they had made camp and the poisoned grub had caught up with him. Damn Miguel! But he too as at fault; too eager to get back to the US, he had not taken precautions enough. Now he was paying the price.

Clay dropped his saddle; it was heavy but had been useful perched high on his left shoulder, offering shade for his head which ached like the worst hang-over he could remember. Likely the aftermath of the stuff Miguel had laced his grub with; his belly was still rumbling and complaining.

He *must* have been ingesting it for the four days the Mexican had led him into this wild country, a little at a time, slowly messing up his brain; otherwise he would have realized that the river *had* to be much closer than the guide had claimed.

Well, there it was now and that stretch of chaparral lifting into low hills beyond looked no different from the miles of the stuff he had forced his way through this last day and a half. Except, over there, it was in Texas.

21

That was what made it different, more attractive then the flesh-ripping, gunshot-crackling brush he had pushed and crawled through. Though the saddle had been useful there, too, thrusting ahead of him, forcing a path.

The Mexican might have put one over on him but he had been too confident, too stupid, or even in too much of a hurry to bother trying to hide his trail.

Well, *why* didn't matter now. From his vantage point Clay could see across the river, the well-used eroded track leading up out of the arroyo carved by yearly floods. That was the way Miguel would have gone, following the known track of fugitives leaving Mexico because they were wanted, or of gringos who had worn out their welcome south of the border, and were risking going back to the *Estados Unidos*.

Well, he could go back, all right – now. Or once he recovered the money from the thieving sonuver of a guide.

Without that money, things might not go so well.

Emory hefted the saddle a little higher on his shoulders and, using the weight of the Henry rifle to give him some balance, began the long slide down the slope towards the beckoning banks of the waist-deep river.

With any luck he would pick up Miguel's campfire in the dusk or, if he had to wait until morning, find his trail. Dragging Emory's mount behind his own pinto, using it as a packhorse, Miguel had left a trail that couldn't be clearer if it had been signposted. That meant he had no fear of Emory surviving the food poisoning and following him.

Surprise! Surprise! You sneaky son of a whore!

The sun had just disappeared behind the hills, outlining the broken-toothed crests with blazing fire that reddened the sky, when the weary, staggering, Emory sat down lumpily, easing his aching, wet-from-the-waist-down body against his saddle. Breathing hard, he decided he would rest a spell and move on after dark if there was enough starlight, make the rest of the climb and hope he could pick up some sign of Miguel's camp. Time wasn't too important now he was at last back on his home ground.

He mopped his forehead, groping for the near-empty canteen, and suddenly froze.

The unmistakable sound of a gunshot came slapping down the darkening slope, bringing him back to full consciousness as he groped for the battered old Henry rifle.

Over the crest the sun was still shining with that golden hue prior to the day's close. Shadows were blurred yet very dark and solid. *And some were moving!*

Clay Emory went to ground fast, leaving the saddle behind a small bunch of rocks as he sprawled on his belly, using knees and elbows to take him just beyond the rocks so he could see better.

It looked like Miguel had run out of luck. Even from up here at this angle, he could see the bloody face with the drooping moustache; the hat was gone, and a good deal of the top of Miguel's head with it.

He pressed tighter against the earth as a man

23

appeared carrying a Winchester, butt warily braced into his hip, finger on the trigger. He played it safe even though it must be damned obvious from his position that Miguel was no danger to him – or anyone else.

Emory's grip on the Henry tightened as the man squatted, reached out and picked up one of the money sacks. His face was shadowed by his hat brim, but, holding his breath, Clay heard him laugh briefly.

'Well, you sure hit the jackpot this time, Miguel, you old thief! If you wasn't so messed up I think I might even kiss you!'

He looked around cursorily, laid down the rifle and began to shake out the contents of the sack on to the ground. Emory growled quietly, involuntarily, and moved his body enough to make the gravel crunch. The killer's head snapped up. He let the sack fall and swept the rifle across his chest as he threw himself sideways and back, taking advantage of the slope, sliding down to a point where he could roll in swiftly behind some of the scattered rocks.

During the slide he'd worked the lever and the rifle crashed just as he squirmed under cover. It was a damn good shot in the circumstances, thought a startled Emory as the lead kicked gravel into his face. He rolled fast, dug in his boot toes and propelled himself behind a mound of dirt packed against a cluster of small boulders. Reacting instinctively, he came up to one knee, the Henry's worn butt jabbing against his shoulder as he triggered. The ancient rimfire cartridge made a dull, flatter sound compared with the up-to-date centrefire ammunition the killer was using. Clay was thankful it had even fired without exploding in the breech.

He rolled again, levering in a fresh load as the man down there raked his cover with three fast, deadly shots. Emory heaved aside, and the dirt under him gave way so that he fell into view, kicking and sliding despite himself. The man with the Winchester laughed, stood up, aiming down for his finishing shot.

The Henry swung wildly across Emory's body and he pulled the trigger. It cracked in that half-hearted sound a rimfire makes compared with the thunder of a centrefire, and the gun jumped from his hands, falling between two rocks. It not only startled him, it startled the killer, and the man stumbled, his shot driving into the ground beside the dead body of Miguel. Emory launched himself headlong, arms reaching for the struggling man. The killer let go the Winchester and dragged his Colt free of leather, swinging it towards Emory.

Clay hurled himself towards Miguel's sagging body, hit him at shoulder level. The fat man tumbled and rolled the couple of feet downslope, fell on top of the gunman. Emory scooped up the Winchester, crouching, levered and fired, all movements instinctive and so fast they were blurred.

The bullet took Miguel's killer high in the chest and hurled his body six feet downslope, to fetch up against a rock with a thud. The Colt slid away from his flailing hand.

Panting, blinking in the smoke-smudged half-light,

Clay Emory jacked one more shell into the Winchester's breech but he saw he wasn't going to need it.

Out of the three men on that slope, he was the only one still alive.

That changed less than half an hour later.

He was gathering what he could use, wondering what to dig a couple of graves with, or should he simply cover the bodies with branches, when he heard twigs crack as if a boot was being placed so as to make as little noise as possible.

He scooped up the Winchester – to hell with the old Henry stuck somewhere amongst the rocks – and found himself facing two shadowy armed men in range clothes, one with a cocked Colt, the other with a carbine.

'Now just don't get too fidgety, *amigo*,' the man with the carbine said; he was short, but wide-shouldered, upper body wedge-shaped where it tapered unexpectedly into a waspish waist. There was no trace of friendliness in the thin face or the narrowed eyes, which seemed pale even in this fading light.

The man with the six-gun was taller, had a high-crowned hat, which added to his height. Rawboned, lantern-jawed, he looked mighty tough, unshaven jowls seeming to heighten the impression of low tolerance and no nonsense.

Emory let the rifle drop, raising his hands out from his sides. 'Easy, boys. I've got no argument with you.'

Shorty spat. 'Not yet.' The carbine poked in the

26

direction of the dead rifleman first, then towards Miguel's sprawled bulk which was now attracting a growing cloud of flies. 'Let's see how things are after you explain these.'

Clay Emory wet his lips. Did these men know the American he had killed with his own gun? Or had Miguel been coming to meet them, maybe? He figured he had to step warily here.

'Start with who you are,' Shorty said curtly, sounding impatient.

'Name's Clay – ton.' Emory added the last part after a brief hesitation. Just in case; he didn't know who these rannies were. They looked like range riders, but could be just Border Rats, looking for easy pickings. 'I've been working in Mexico and I hired him to bring me here.' He gestured to the dead Mexican.

'Poor old Miguel, huh?' the tall man said, causing Emory to stiffen. So they did know the Mexican.

' "Poor old Miguel", my foot!' growled Emory. 'That son of a bitch tried to poison me! Fed me stuff in my grub and damn near killed me.'

The two men exchanged glances. Shorty replied. 'Now why would he do that? You have somethin' he wanted badly?' He gestured to the open saddle-bags. 'That a leetle *dinero* I see showin' there near the flap, mebbe?'

Clay cursed himself for not buckling the flap again but it was too late now. 'That's money I earned. An', yeah, the Mex figured he could use it better'n I could.'

The two men exchanged glances again. 'You know

Miguel was that way inclined, Tower?'

The tall one shook his head. 'No. Never did. But I never knew him as good as you, Short.'

Shorty nodded, flicked his pale gaze to Emory. 'Well, Clayton, I have to say I've knowed Miguel for some years and he was always a light-fingered, money-grubbin' bastard.' He paused, smiling crookedly at Clay Emory's look of total agreement. 'But likeable,' he added and chuckled. 'Find that last part had to believe, huh?'

'No-ooo,' Emory admitted. 'He seemed "likeable" enough when I first hired him. I ain't what you call a greenhorn, but I didn't figure he was about to jump me along the trail.'

'Shouldn't've flashed your money around. How much, by the way?' Tower seemed genuinely interested and Emory felt his belly tighten.

'Never mind how much. Just take it that I sweated my guts out for nigh on two years to make it. And I'm taking it to where it rightfully belongs.'

'Ooooo,' Tower said, pursing his prunelike lips. 'He do sound tough, don't he, Short?'

'He do. But I'd still like to know how much it made Miguel figure it was worthwhile poisonin' a gringo for.'

At least they seemed to have believed that much of his story. . . .

'Never mind how much is there! It's mine and that's all that matters.' Clay flicked his gaze towards the Winchester, wishing he had propped it against the rock beside him instead of dropping it.

'Uh-huh,' Shorty mouthed half-aloud, eyes narrowing again.

'Who are you fellers, anyway? Local cowboys?'

'Could say so. Lookin' for mavericks. We're outriders for the Broken D spread. Heard of it?'

Clay frowned, stiffened but tried to cover. 'Hell, didn't think I was this far east! That's Big Mal Donovan's place, ain't it?'

'Yeah. And that other feller you killed, yonder, is Slim Norton, wrangler of the Rectangle 5. Which just happens to be Broken D's neighbour.'

He stopped and there was something in the way he said the words that deepened Clay's frown.

'You – er – havin' rustler trouble, mebbe?'

'Mebbe,' cut in Tower. 'Or somethin' like it.' He paused, then added quietly: 'We ain't havin' much luck locatin' any mavericks on our range. Anythin' we find has already been branded, not always with Rectangle 5, but sometimes.'

'Like – someone's moving in ahead of you, chousing the mavericks and slappin' their own brand on quick-smart?'

'You seem to know the kinda deal!' Shorty snapped.

'Nothin' new in it. Rival spreads've worked it for years. Hey, wait! You don't think I. . . ? Judas priest, I'd never set eyes on that Norton *hombre* till he started shooting at me!' He flicked his gaze from one to the, other.

It was mighty clear they didn't believe him.

'I think he might've been comin' to meet Miguel,' Emory added quickly. 'Or someone. He seemed to be waiting a bit along the trail and he had field glasses. He must've seen Miguel counting my *dinero* and figured, why share it with a Mex?'

Tower spat and Shorty pursed his lips once more. 'I dunno, Tower. He's pretty damn glib. And he only says the money belongs to him. You prove it, Clayton?'

Emory shook his head. 'Not if I didn't have to. And sure not to you.'

That brought knowing smiles to their faces. 'Ah-hah! That kinda *dinero* huh?' Tower spat again, jerked his gun barrel. 'Short, I reckon we better have Mal take a look at this *hombre.*'

Shorty snapped his head round, didn't look pleased.

'You know how he's a stickler for law an' order right now,' Tower said somewhat irritably. 'I mean, he musta broke every damn law ever written to build up Broken D but now he's got religion, wants a lily-white background so's he can marry in what he calls "a gratifyin' manner". I don't wanna see that one-eyed stare on me! Sooner look down the muzzle of a twelve-gauge.'

Shorty hesitated, nodded reluctantly. 'Does he have to know about it?' He gestured to the saddle-bags.

Tower snorted. 'You think Clayton won't tell him if he can get us in bad and himself in good with Big Mal?'

'Would you do that?' Shorty asked, and there was an unstated threat in his voice.

'Damn right!'

Shorty lifted his Colt. 'Want to bet?'

'Easy, Short!' Tower snapped.

'Hell, Towers. There's the damn Rio, a frog's leap away! No one knows about this except us! We could be across in less than a hour, these bodies hid under a cutbank, an'. . . .'

The tall man was shaking his head slowly before the other had stopped speaking. 'Temptin', Short. But wouldn't be worth it. Not if it means you'd have to keep lookin' over your shoulder for Big Mal Donovan – and one time find him there!'

Shorty stared, then swallowed. There could have been a mild sheen of sweat on his round face.

'And you would,' Emory said abruptly, so that they swung their gazes on to him.

'The hell would you know about it?' Shorty growled, but his face straightened when Emory said,

'Not a lot – except Big Mal has an interest in this here money, too.'

Both cowboys stiffened. Shorty blinked, trying to come to terms with Emory's words. 'You – know Big Mal?'

Clay smiled crookedly. 'Well enough to be taking his share to him.'

'Ju-das *Priest*!' gasped Shorty, eyes widening as he looked at Tower. 'What the hell've we walked into here, Tower?'

The tall man kept his hard stare on Clay. 'I wouldn't like even to hazard a guess, Short. But I do know it's somethin' I ain't prepared to take a chance on!' He jerked his gun at Emory. 'Turn around so's we can tie your hands.'

'Hey!' Clay said, but the gun still threatened and he

31

hesitated only a second longer, then started to turn, watching warily.

But while Tower returned his gaze he didn't see Shorty swing his Colt. He felt the barrel hit him across the side of the head an instant before somebody blew out the candle.

His last conscious thought was that he hoped he had read the name right on that crudely-drawn map that had led him to the money.

If not. . . ? But the blackness swallowed him before the thought finished forming.

CHAPTER 3

BROKEN D

Clay Emory had never seen the legendary Big Mal Donovan but he recognized him immediately when the door of the shed where he had awakened, opened and a big shape ducked inside.

The rancher couldn't straighten fully, must have been six feet five or six, and the shed's shingle roof sloped towards the rear where Emory lay with a throbbing head. Donovan looked as tough as his legend claimed and the eyepatch he wore over the empty left socket made him an intimidating figure. The moustache, darker than the thinning, grey-streaked hair on his head, was kind of ragged, growing over old scar tissue: an ancient wound from an Apache tomahawk which had left him with a slight lisp.

Shorty and Tower crowded in behind him, both with faces carefully composed in the light of the lamp held by the long-faced Tower.

'You're Clayton?' Donovan's voice was deep, drawling like a Texan with ancestors going back before the Alamo.

'Yeah. You Donovan?' Clay winced; it hurt to talk.

'*Mister* Donovan!' growled Shorty, quivering with anger. 'You lyin' sonuver! You dunno the boss at all! I oughta. . . .'

The big rancher held up one huge hand and Shorty fell quiet on the instant.

Big Mal was wearing a six-gun in a casual manner, pushed around towards his right hip, but the very apparent carelessness didn't convince Clay that Donovan couldn't get the Colt out and working in a flash if he so wanted. There were legends about that, too. 'Boys've told me your story, Clayton. I guess trash like Miguel had to run outta luck sometime. Slim Norton's no loss, neither, not to me, leastways. Nor to Mattie Carr I'd guess. Thing is, do we b'lieve your story or not? That ain't really a hard question to decide, since you already lied about knowing me.'

'Said that to protect myself from these two jugheads. They aimed to take the money and run across the Rio, after putting a bullet in me.'

'That's a goddamn lie!' shouted Shorty very quickly.

'Yeah, he's lyin', boss,' Tower cut in smartly.

Clay gave Donovan a straight look. 'Believe what you like. Makes no nevermind to me. *I* know it happened how I said. Lyin' about you due a share of the *dinero* was the only way I could see to save my skin.'

Shorty and Tower seemed to shrivel under the glinting stare from Donovan's single eye. 'Well. They ain't

34

real bad boys, and I can savvy the temptation, but I hardly need a share of my own money! Leave it for now.' Then his reasonable tone suddenly hardened as he looked at his men. 'I'll get the straight of it later.'

Both cowboys looked pale and Tower stretched his neck as if his shirt collar was too tight, although it was already unbuttoned.

'Tell me your version,' Donovan said, turning to Clay Emory.

Clay's head was throbbing and his wrists were still bound. He held them up for the rancher to see and Donovan nodded curtly to Shorty who drew his hunting knife and cut the cords.

Emory told his story succinctly. When he had finished, Big Mal waited a few moments, then said: 'You started halfway through, didn't you?'

'Told you all you need to know.'

'Bo-o-ss!' Tower gritted, hand dropping to gunbutt.

Mal Donovan lifted a hand without looking at the tall man. 'How about why you were in Mexico in the first place? And *how* did you get a hold of that money?'

Clay rubbed his wrists for a spell in silence. Then said, 'Did a little mercenary work with the *rebeldes* till it got too hot, then hooked up with Mustang Speers's outfit. He was collectin' a thousand horses at the time, contracted for delivery to the Mexican cavalry post at Comargo, on the Rio Conchos. Everyone who put in broncs was up for a share on percentage, according to how many they brought to the drive.'

'You're not tryin' to tell me all that money was your share!'

'Partly. About five thousand, mebbe a mite more. I put in a couple hundred hosses. They were paying thirty-five a head in Mexico, delivered to Comargol, against a lousy sixteen bucks from the US Army, fully broke an' trail-ready. Mexico was far the better deal.'

Donovan's gaze was steady. 'Must've taken quite a time to get two hundred mustangs broke for a long trail – a one-man outfit.'

'Had a pard, Chuck Murphy. Struck trouble driving south. The rebs got wind of Speers supplying remounts to the Government. We had – aw, must've been six, seven raids along the way. Murphy was killed in one of 'em.'

'Which put more *dinero* in your pocket, eh?'

Clay held the single eye's hard stare. 'That was our deal: survivor got the lot. You ought to savvy that kinda deal; from what I hear it'd be a whole heap better than some of the shady ones you made when you were buildin' this place.'

'Hey! That's it!' snapped Tower, starting forward, but one look from Donovan and he said, 'But he's sassin' you!'

'Just letting me know I don't scare him.' Big Mal smiled thinly, the black moustache twitching slightly. 'Not many men I can say that about.'

'You're from a different time, Donovan. Your kind have had their day, some are still havin' it, I guess. But now the law is coming into its own. Kinda . . . restrictin', huh?'

Donovan inclined his head, showing some surprise. 'I reached that conclusion a spell back. Never figured no lousy trail bum would point it out to me, though.'

'Drifting around, you get lots of time to think.'

'All right, Clayton, or whatever your name is. . . .' A pause, but it got no response from Emory. 'S'pose I b'lieve you. Your share of the horse trade was around five thousand.

'But Shorty tells me there was the best part of *ten* thousand in your saddle-bags, mebbe more – a lot of it in gold. You got a story to go with that, too?'

Emory laughed briefly. 'A story! Yeah, OK, I'll tell you a story, give you the details, and you can chew on 'em – or spit 'em out. Be damned if I care which.'

'By God! How old are you? Thirty, or more?' Clay grunted. 'Just wondering how the hell you've managed to live for so damn long!'

'By always bein' polite to my elders.'

Donovan's face was like a black thundercloud, but only momentarily. Then he grinned, not a nice grin, and one just big enough to acknowledge that Clay Emory – 'Clayton' as he knew him – was that rare thing on the frontier these days: he was his own man, and fear, servility or backing down were not words in his vocabulary.

'Well, what the hell you waitin' for? Tell me how come a saddle bum like you can earn – or come by – enough honest money to set him up for life.'

Clay smiled thinly. 'I didn't exactly say it was "honest" money.'

In the sudden silence that ensued, Emory started to talk before they asked too many more questions.

*

'It was the biggest horse drive south since the end of the War – through country that normally supports nothing but a few armadillos, parakeets and shingle-back lizards – with an occasional jaguar or bobcat thrown in. . . .'

A drove of 1,000 horses; 4,000 pounding hoofs and rumbling bellies, plus those of the remuda, required a lot of grass and water.

Because of the amount necessary for the big herd, Mustang Speers made the decision that those who had brought in their horses to make up the numbers would be responsible for those animals.

In other words, it was up to the small-herd contributors to find graze and water for their own horses each sundown, even if it was some miles from where the main body of horses were settling in for the night.

That way the combined herd would not eat out a huge section of the southern trail.

It made good sense.

But it wasn't a popular decision, and two ranchers withdrew, aiming to make their own way down to the Army post at Comargo.

'We'll go it alone and dicker for our own price,' one stubborn man named Cowley growled belligerently.

Speers was a small man, but tougher than many believed possible, until they locked horns with him.

'If that's your decision cut out your broncs – and make damn sure they're only ones wearin' your brands.'

That brought a violent response but the two quitters were surprised when Speers laid them both out with a swinging axe handle and gave them till noon to be on their way.

'You're damn fools,' he told them as they held water-soaked rags against the lumps on their heads. 'You're on your own now. Don't expect no back-up from me when the *bandidos* come after you.'

The very next day one of the riders Speers had sent back to make sure Cowley and his men were OK (but he would never admit that that was the true reason) rode in hell for leather to report that they'd found Cowley and all his men dead, shot and mutilated, the horses gone.

There were no other quitters, but Speers didn't change his orders: 'Find your own graze and water each sundown. Rendezvous at my camp one hour after sunup to join the main herd for the next day's drive. There'll be no waitin' for latecomers.'

That was how it was, though Speers did send back a couple of extra nighthawks to help watch for raiders.

It seemed to work for a few nights; then there was a big raid on the main herd, which scattered the horses to hell and gone and left dead and wounded men from both sides.

While Speers and his men rode all over the country, retrieving the mounts, the raiders hit the small herders, confident that resistance would be minimal.

Clay Emory and Chuck Murphy had grazed their herd that night on slopes above a creek, watering the horses first before driving them, reluctantly, back to the short grass higher up. The idea had been to let them fill their bellies with water and so eat less.

Sometimes it worked.

But the raiders hit them while Murphy and one of the two nighthawks they had hired, just working for wages, kept an eye on the herd. Clay and the other nighthawk were to relieve them about four o'clock.

But it was pitch dark when the rattle of gunfire and screams and the thunder of stampeding hoofs woke them. Clay pulled on his boots, snatched the rifle he had been sleeping with and ran for his ground-hitched sorrel.

'C'mon, Buck!' he yelled at the sleepy nighthawk. He leapt on to the boulder beside the startled mount and dropped on to its bare back. His heels rammed home and his mouth let wild epithets fly as he wheeled the snorting animal using the hackamore, racing upslope.

There were a lot of gun flashes above, mostly rifles by the sounds of them. Hatless, the wind cut at his eyes and filled them with water, blurring his vision as he shot out of a small arroyo and saw the milling raiders ahead, driving his herd across the slope. Buck came surging up and made up for his previous tardiness by holding on with his knees while he worked the lever of his Winchester.

Clay saw two men go down, looked for Murphy even as he shot a third man, though the Mexican only slumped forward, did not fall from the saddle. Where the hell was Chuck!

Irritably he brushed the wetness from his eyes, too late to see the rope stretched between two tall rocks. Later, he figured he had missed that Mex, that the man hadn't slumped in the saddle, only ducked low to get beneath the rope he and his comrades had rigged to discourage pursuit.

It swept Clay Emory out of the saddle, catching him across the shoudlers and tumbling him half down the slope before he came to a halt, dazed, clothes torn, bleeding from a graze over his left eye.

Staggering up the slope, bitterly cursing as he heard the raiders driving off his horses, he found Buck draped over a boulder, his skull shattered when the damn rope trap had flung him from his racing horse.

The next body he found was that of Chuck Murphy; he had had the back of his head blown off. The nighthawk who had been with him he found in a gully, trying to crawl out, head bleeding and holding his side with a bloody hand.

Mustang Speers wasn't as hard as he made out. He sent three men with Clay to go after the raiders. The trail was easy to follow and the ambush the raiders set up was just too obvious to be effective.

He had two of Speers's men keep them occupied with lots of shooting while he got around behind them: two men with loaded guns laid out beside them, ready for their targets. Except they only had two below that they could see.

Clay came in from above and behind them. He slipped at the last second, a trickle of gravel alerting the killers, even as he jumped down from his rock. He landed in a crouch and did his shooting from that position, lever clashing as the rifle blasted. One Mexican seemed to leap back as the bullet caught him

41

in the throat and he died in a bloody welter that lasted even after Clay had killed his companion. There was still a little life left in him and the Speers men found Clay standing with a foot on the dying man's chest, hot rifle muzzle an inch from the staring eyes.

'Where they takin' my hosses?' Emory demanded, pressing the rifle muzzle against the man's forehead now. 'Tell me and I'll put you outta your misery.'

The man only shook his head, made some kind of feeble gesture with one bloody hand and choked on his own blood.

'I think he was pointin', Clay,' said one of the riders, Banning. 'That way.'

There was a veritable wall of screening brush and it showed sign of recent, rough passage. They went in afoot, guns ready, but there was no need. There was only one more raider who had been left with the horses now grazing in a hollow.

He was dead, dried blood on his two wounds telling them that he had been shot during the night raid.

Clay's mouth was dry from talking and Donovan had him taken into one end of the big bunkhouse, where Shorty slammed down a pot of coffee in front of him.

After the first cup, and while another was cooling, with a shot of whiskey added, Clay nodded his thanks to Donovan, who was regarding him strangely.

'Your herd was intact?' he asked, deep voice sounding edgy – and sceptical.

'Mostly. Lost seven or eight.'

'Goddamn! You're either a liar or one lucky cuss!'

'Said before, I don't care which you believe. Your opinion don't matter spit to me. Just go easy on that "liar" tag. I've told you what happened.'

Donovan's one eye was narrowed, his whole attitude one of growing exasperation.'And. . . ?'

Clay sipped his coffee, looked through the steam at the big rancher. 'It was obviously the camp the raiders had been using for some time. We buried the dead, includin' Murphy, had a look through the Mexes' things. Speers's men took a lot of personal stuff, but I settled for a couple of old but nicely carved Spanish saddle-bags. They were heavy, but Speers had sent a man out to hurry us up so I never had time to look in 'em right then. We got goin', finished the drive to Comargo and eventually got paid off.'

Donovan waited and Tower and Shorty moved impatiently. Clay asked for a smoke and the rancher surprised him by offering him a short cigar from a leather case with a silver clasp.

The smoke was aromatic and smooth. 'Obliged, Donovan. I know what you're waiting to hear: where did I get gold money wrapped in hundred-dollar bills, right?'

'That's easy. It was in the fancy saddle-bags you took from the Mexes' camp.'

Clay smiled. 'Nope.' He paused for effect, enjoying this now. 'Oh, there was money in the bags, all right, gold *pesos*, giving them the weight: several hundred bucks. I gave Speers's men the choice: the money or the map.'

'Map?' snapped Donovan, straightening abruptly.

'Uh-huh. I found it stuffed away in the bottom of one of the saddle-bags, tucked under the lining. I had a hunch about it, seeing as it had been hidden like that. Well, Speers's men chose the money, of course, and after I got paid off in Comargo, I played my hunch and followed the map. It led me to an old iron-bound strongbox buried in the back of a cave. There were a helluva lot of gold *pesos* in that box. Could've paid for a lot of guns.'

He paused again and they looked at him expectantly. ' "Could've"?' asked Donovan quietly, that single eye steady and piercing.

Clay spread his hands, trying to look innocent. 'Well, I couldn't let that happen, could I?'

'So you took it.'

Emory studied the big rancher carefully. 'What would you've done?'

That ragged moustache didn't move till a long breath had passed. Then it twitched and Big Mal said,

'Why, if it'd been me I reckon Broken D'd be about one third bigger by now. All fully drained land, too, and so many cattle you wouldn't be able to see the grass for 'em.'

Clay smiled, nodding. 'That's what I figured, goin' on your past performances . . . and a place on the map, along the Rio, Manzano Point, that had a name beside it – Broken D.'

The big rancher's single eye glared coldly at Clay, who said, 'I wondered why Mex rebels would mark a remote corner of your spread on their map?'

Donovan ignored that completely. 'With that kinda

money, I'd spread Broken D over half this corner of
Texas. Could even secede, make it a separate territory.
Somethin' like – hell, why not? "Donovan's Domain"!
Think that'd be a mite too much? You know what I
mean?'

Clay felt his face grow hot. Donovan was telling him
he was aiming to take the money! And that meant Clay
would have to die: no witnesses.

He started to get to his feet quickly, but that Colt
that had seemed to be a long way from Donovan's gun
hand, was suddenly pointing at him, the hammer
already at full cock.

'You got two choices, Clayton. Sit down – or be shot
down.'

CHAPTER 4

WHERE DEAD MEN LAY

Clay wondered where the rest of the Broken D crew were, but suddenly had other things much more urgent to think about.

Donovan's gun wavered around in a short arc as he stared at Emory across the table. Shorty and Tower hovered in the background, each with a look of quiet uncertainty on his face. This, too, puzzled Clay, but then Donovan said,

'Figure you know me pretty well, huh?'

'Not me. I've heard plenty of talk but I've never found that you learn much real stuff about anyone by listening to "talk".'

'You could be right. Tell me just what you figure you know.'

Clay frowned but shrugged. 'Guess I know as much as anyone else who's never met you before. There was that dime novel about you that some *Harper's Weekly* reporter wrote.' Donovan said nothing, just nodded gently. 'Called it *Wild Mal Donovan*, made you a cross between that Limey outlaw, Robin Hood, and our own Deadwood McLaine. You want the truth, I thought Deadwood came out the better character, although he left a string of dead men from here to Canada. Don't recollect hearing anythin' about you ever giving anything at all to the poor, neither – like that Hood *hombre.*'

Donovan's face was stern, his single eye narrowed and drilled into Emory. The gun barrel moved in another short arc, crashed against the bullet scar on Clay's left cheek and sent him tumbling out of his chair.

As Emory groped dazedly to his feet, face bleeding, Donovan said, quite amicably, 'Uh-huh. Well, if a man wants somethin' bad enough, he goes out and gets it. That's my philosophy.'

'At any price? Even runnin' guns across the Rio?'

'Up to him, ain't it? He wants it badly enough he won't let *anythin'* stand in his way.'

'Yeah, well that writer got you nailed all right. Everyone knows for a fact you shot down three Mexes who were s'posed to be guardin' the northern line of land claimed by a Don Roberto Alvado, who was some wrong-side-of-the-blanket kin to one of the Spanish royalty, somethin' like that.'

He thought Donovan was going to hit him again, but the gun merely jerked an inch. The rancher smiled crookedly as Clay reared back. 'Son of a bitch claimed almost a third of North Mexico! Too damn

47

much for any man, let alone some greaser!'

'So you killed his men and took over that part of his land and cattle, and now you are well on the way to owning one helluva big slice of Texas.'

Donovan seemed to regard Clay more warily now.

'It'll get bigger! And I goddamn well worked for what I have! Rounded up wild cattle to build my herds, fought Injuns *and* Alvado's *guarda* he had the hide to send across the Rio to wipe me out. I kept that part of the border clear of gun runnin' and smugglin' and slavin' for years. I was even mentioned in Congress for doing it. I damn well *earned* my right to Broken D!'

'But it wasn't enough was it?' Clay said astutely.

Big Mal's baleful eye glinted but it was barely noticeable between the fast narrowing lids. His knuckles whitened about the six-gun and Shorty and Tower tensed.

So did Clay. 'You wanted reward that you could hold. You wanted to *count*, good ol' hard cash, and a little power wouldn't go amiss.' Donovan didn't shoot. Clay licked his lips and added. 'You still ain't satisfied. You want it bigger and better. Guns're a fast way of makin' big money.'

There followed a long silence that stretched out and made Shorty cough and Tower shuffle his feet. Donovan didn't even seem to breathe as that deadly stare held to Emory's face.

'You got more brains than I figured. We mighta gotten along pretty good, you and me.'

Clay tensed at the rancher's words. 'Mebbe we still can.'

48

Big Mal shook his head slowly. 'You're either some kinda lawman or just too damn smart for your own good. I don't like smartasses.'

Clay flicked his gaze to the bodyguards. 'So I see.'

Donovan lifted his left hand without looking at his men and they swallowed their protests. 'OK. I've reached my decision. I'll take the rest of that *dinero*.'

Emory raised his eyebrows. 'The *rest* of it? Hell, you've got it all now!'

The big head moved slowly. 'I don't think so. There must've been more in that strongbox than you let them fellers grab. You'd've made sure you kept a damn good share.'

The big muzzle of the six-gun suddenly rose and clipped Clay across the jaw. He rocked in the chair, almost fell but grabbed at the edge of the table, face throbbing eyes spinning, more blood oozing.

'You could be one helluva mess by the time we finish this conversation, Clayton.'

But Donovan gave him time to recover his senses. By then, Clay had made his decision: no use trying to tell Big Mal there really was no more money. The rancher was convinced there was more, so. . . .

'We-ell. Maybe I wanted a stake to get goin' myself.' The rancher snorted, glanced at his men as if to say *See? I was right!* 'Hell, it ain't fair you take the lot!'

'I'll tell you what's fair.' Big Mal leaned across the table. 'What I say is fair. *Comprende?*'

Clay eased back, hesitated and reached carefully for a kerchief to hold against his swelling, bleeding face. 'OK. You got me cold-decked!'

'You can believe that. Now you just prove me right by tellin' me where you got the rest of my *dinero* hid.'

'Your *dinero*!'

'Mine. You wanta play it tough, go right ahead. These boys are good cowmen, but I gotta tell you they're a helluva lot better at makin' a man suffer pure hell than they are runnin' steers.'

Shorty and Tower smiled crookedly.

Clay sighed. 'We'll have to go back to where we left Miguel an' that other feller, Norton.'

'Why?'

'I stashed some of the money there.'

'Just say where and they'll go get it.'

Clay shook his head. 'I did it in a hurry when I heard Norton comin' in. I was amongst some rocks, but I had to crawl all over the slope, tradin' lead with him, didn't know where the hell I was by the time it was over. I'll know the rocks again, though, when I see 'em. But I can't explain exactly where they are.'

'He's stallin', boss,' growled Tower.

' 'Course he is,' Donovan agreed. He stood and motioned them to a corner some distance from where Clay sat dabbing at his face. All three watched him as Donovan said quietly, 'I don't want his body found anywhere near here. Go back to where he killed the others, and get my money.' He added grimly: 'And leave him there. Savvy?'

They nodded, waited for him to say more, but he just stared with that one glittering eye. Tower was first to smile. He nudged Shorty with an elbow and winked down at him.

Suddenly, Shorty smiled too.

In fact, Clay Emory was the only one who wasn't smiling. He was damned if he could see any reason to.

They knew he didn't have a hope in hell of surviving this ride.

Trouble was, he more than half-believed it himself.

Shorty and Tower seemed to think that it was, as far as they were concerned, Clay's last ride, so they might as well get some fun out of it while they could.

His hands were tied to the saddle horn and every so often the Broken D men would take it in turns to ride in close and hook him a blow in his kidneys, or deliver a swipe across the back of the head, a dizzying slap on the ears, a poke in the midriff.

He was bleeding, aching and raging mad by the time they crossed the narrow creek and started the climb up the steep slope to where the bodies of Miguel and Norton lay.

Clay spat some blood, used his tongue to probe at a loose tooth and spat a little more. By accident or design some splashed on Shorty's scuffed and dusty left boot. The man swore and bared his teeth as he bad-mouthed Emory and swung a blow at his head. Clay ducked and dodged the blow that came at him on the return.

This incensed Shorty and he drew his six-gun, swung it at Clay's already battered face. Clay didn't quite get out of the way and the foresight cut him on the cheek. Shorty seemed satisfied to see more blood flow, looked at Tower for appreciation.

51

'Leave somethin' to kick around when we get there,' the tall man growled.

Shorty snorted and Clay said, thickly, 'What was that Slim Norton doing up there, anyway?'

The Broken D men stared, Tower frowning. He glanced at Shorty and shrugged. His companion said,

'Aw, it's him been usin' the runnin' iron on Broken D mavericks. Bet if we looked in one of them hidden draws, we'd find enough one-time mavericks to bring Mal's count up to scratch. Slim was a slimy snake; on the dodge, I've heard.'

'Yeah. Likely you're right.' Tower stretched out and knocked Clay's hat off. 'Now you shut up till we get there – and then the only time you open your mouth is to tell us where you stashed the money. Savvy?'

Emory said nothing, swallowed a little blood, spat some more. His eyes were like twin gun barrels but the others were too elated at having him to beat up and eventually kill to heed any warning this might give.

The buzzards and some four-legged animals – likely coyotes – had been at the corpses. The three of them dismounted and stood around looking for a few minute. Then Clay held out his bound wrists.

'The hell you doin'? You can find where you stashed the *dinero* without your hands bein' free.'

'Mebbe. But I kicked some rocks over the bags and I'll have to move 'em to get at the dough.'

Shorty frowned and looked at Tower. The latter gave it some thought, then took out his knife and cut the bonds. He got a kick out of seeing Clay swing his arms and dance a jig as the blood began circulating through his numbed hands.

'Hurry it up!' growled Tower, sheathing the knife.

'Hell. Can't even feel my hands!'

'Hurry – it – up!' Tower's six-gun whispered out of leather and the hammer clicked to full cock.

Clay held up his tingling hands in a pushing-away gesture. 'OK, OK! Gimme a minute while I look around and see if I can find the place.'

'Not "if"!' snapped Shorty. '*Find* it! And pronto!'

Clay nodded, again making that 'gimme a break' gesture with his hands, which were getting some feeling back now. But he didn't let on; he kept shaking them from the wrists, grimacing as if returning blood flow was hurting, to the great amusement of the others. They sat down on a rock, where Shorty rolled a cigarette and stuck it between Tower's lips, rolled another for himself and lit both smokes.

While they were occupied with this Emory scouted around the rocks, occasionally moving one a little, shaking his head, moving on. He looked up, worry and a growing fear plain on his face. 'I – I don't see the rocks. . . .'

'You better!' Shorty's six-gun covered him, hammer cocked. 'Or we'll be pilin' rocks on your corpse!'

Clay pressed his hands into his aching back, grimacing. 'You fellers play . . . rough! Listen, what happens if – when – I find the money?'

Tower and Shorty exchanged a glance, both trying not to laugh. The tall man said,

'Why, Mal just said to leave you. Guess all he wants is the *dinero*. So, looks like you'll be able to ride off.'

Clay's face brightened. 'Hey! That's good to know. Ahha! I think this is the place!'

He dropped between some rocks and crouched down. The two Broken D men stood up, tense now with the prospect of success.

Then suddenly Clay was spinning, dropping to one knee, holding the old Henry rifle that had jumped from his grip when he had been shooting it out with Slim Norton. He had not tried to retrieve it at the time, but had scooped up Miguel's Winchester and. . . .

Now, the battered butt of the Henry was braced against his hip and the old loose lever clanked and wobbled as it jacked cartridges up from the rust-spotted under-barrel magazine. He hoped he had saved shells that would fire from what Miguel had left.

The flat, dull crack of the rimfire ammunition wasn't dramatic in the mid-morning mountain air, but the big, slow, hammering bullets were just as deadly as modern projectiles when they reached their target. Shorty went down first, his thick chest an easy mark. The heavy slug crushed-in his sternum, picked him up and slammed him over a rock. He rolled off and his body hit Tower in the backs of his legs, making him stagger. His six-gun exploded, drowning out Clay's next two shots – his last.

Both bullets missed Tower, one fanning his ear. He twisted wildly, dropped his pistol and made an unco-ordinated wild dive for it.

Clay worked the lever but it jammed halfway and he saw Tower's hand closing over the butt of the Colt. He hurled the useless Henry and followed it through, stumbling but finding a firm place for his feet, and launched himself bodily at the tall man.

They collided, breath bursting from both their bodies. Clay locked his arms around Tower and they rolled out of the rocks, began to slide down the slope, kicking and punching awkwardly. Tower bared his teeth and Emory could feel his right hand fumbling at something. Just as he realized the man was drawing his hunting knife, Tower broke his grip and the blade hissed out of leather.

Clay kicked free and rolled to one side but continued to slide downslope. Tower, too, was still sliding, but he jammed his boots against a deadfall, lunging at Emory who was spread-eagled now. The blade swept around in a flashing arc. Clay yelled as it ripped through his shirt and down over his ribs. Blood flowed and pain seared up into his neck.

Shocked by the sudden trauma, he blinked, felt himself slowing. Then Tower reared over him, knife hand raised and teeth bared with effort. The steel plunged. Clay wrenched his head aside, felt the flat of the cold metal against the side of his neck. *Judas! Too damn close!*

Adrenalin surged. His knees came around and he kicked out savagely. His boots took the forward-lunging Tower in the face and the man's head jerked back violently. He turned the knife edge on and tried to slash across Clay's exposed throat. Emory jammed fingers in the man's eyes and Tower, clawing at his face, let out a scream that could have doubled as a

Comanche war whoop.

Then both men dropped over the low bank into the shallow creek.

Water churned and choked them. They wrenched their heads free. Blood trickled from Tower's eyes, but he still gripped the big-bladed knife, raised it for the killing strike as he got the upper position, holding Clay's head under with one hand spread across the battered face. The knife descended.

Clay's desperately groping hand found an apple-sized rock. He swung it up with all that remained of his waning strength and felt his arm jar, heard a pulpy sound, and suddenly Tower was rolling limply away from him. The knife splashed into the water, sank immediately.

Clay reared to a sitting position, in time to see that the killer's head was all lopsided and out of shape, bleeding red smoke and grey matter into the water.

Gagging, left hand trying to hold his burning side, Clay floundered and splashed to his knees, crab-walked to the bank, but had no strength to crawl out.

He simply folded his upper body over the crumbling edge on to the short grass, and stayed in that position, gulping air, heart hammering, blood pouring from the knife wounds.

His world became a mass of whirling, wildly blending colours that were rapidly lost in a blanket of grey that suddenly turned black as it enveloped him.

CHAPTER 5

MOUNTAIN GRAVEYARD

Mal Donovan locked himself in his office and counted the money from the Spanish saddle-bags. He was mighty pleased with the result: it totalled around $12,000, give or take a few bucks – a few hundred, even.

It was all his, anyway; the rebs must've had it ready to pay for the next shipment of guns. So this was good, easy profit!

It would be enough to get him the Saddlebacks again, and add Turnabout Creek to Broken D. *Then* he would really be someone to reckon with in this part of Texas – spread a few dollars in the right place and they might even name it 'Donovan County'. His ego was towering.

He was standing by the dusty window now, chuckling at the thought; suddenly his dream evaporated as he saw the rider coming into the yard at a fast clip, skidding his big chestnut gelding to a crashing halt by the corrals. A cowhand near by stopped braiding a leather hackamore and blinked as the rider quit the saddle and tossed him the reins of his hard-ridden chestnut.

'Look after him!' the rider snapped.

Before the cowhand could catch the reins and reach up to pat the snorting horse the rider was already sprinting towards the house. He was a tall, lean man with long limbs, and those corduroy-clad legs were a blur as he leapt on to the veranda. He had his hand raised to knock on the office door when it jerked open and Big Mal stood there, arms akimbo, a six-foot-five thunderstorm brewing on the spot.

'The *hell* are you doin' back here, so soon?'

Reece McCoy, Donovan's personal bodyguard – read 'gunfighter' – lifted a finger, swallowing as he tried to catch his breath. He had a narrow face with a big hawklike nose that seemed to chop the air as he pushed past his boss into the office. Big Mal slammed the door, turning fast.

'What is it?' he asked in an even voice, knowing by now that McCoy must be bearing news he wouldn't want to hear.

'Mal. It's like a graveyard up there!'

Donovan's single eye narrowed and drilled into him with almost physical force. 'You see Shorty and Tower?'

'Dead. So's Slim Norton and that greaser border rat, Miguel Delesandro. Blood everywhere.'

'Clayton?' Big Mal asked very quietly.

'I think some of it's his blood. Reckon Tower used his knife on him but somehow got his head smashed in with a rock. Not pretty! Shorty'd been shot to hell.'

'Get on with it! Where's Clayton now?'

'Gone. Looks like he managed to get on a horse, but he's bleedin' a helluva lot. Guess Tower sliced him up good. But seems he can still ride.'

'You didn't trail him?'

McCoy lifted a hand and glanced towards a clear bottle of green-tinged liquid on the end of the desk.

'Could use a touch of the Demon, Mal.'

Donovan irritably waved him to help himself. The gunfighter pulled the cork with his teeth, spat it out and drank a long draught, gasping with open mouth, squeezing his eyes shut as a few tears welled. He wiped the back of a hand across his purplish lips. '*Man*! That really *hits*!'

It was a brew that Donovan distilled himself on the Broken D; he had even fought in court for the privilege, claiming he used an authorized-pattern still and that as long as he didn't market the potent brew, and drank it himself or offered it to any companion he might choose, he wasn't breaking any laws. To his surprise the court agreed. The 'product' quickly earned itself the name of the Demon: its high alcohol content gave an almost instant boost to a jaded man, and could help light a campfire in a full gale. Big Mal grabbed the bottle now and rammed the cork back in. 'You were saying. . . ?' he prompted tightly.

'Yeah. Well, I tracked Clayton a little way, Mal,

59

enough to see he was headed into the foothills. Rectangle 5's workin' a round-up camp down there right now.'

'Not likely Clayton'd know that.'

McCoy shook his head. 'I found the horses that the others must've rode, but not one with a Rectangle 5 brand, that would've belonged to Slim Norton.'

'Then if that's what Clayton's riding, it'll take him right back to the damn round-up camp!'

'I reckon. I rode back to see what you want to do.'

Donovan snatched the bottle and took a big slug himself. His single eye glittered as the Demon rampaged through his system. 'Have my horse saddled – and get a fresh mount for yourself.'

McCoy frowned. 'Hell! I got time to get somethin' to eat? I been ridin' without grub or water for—'

'You got time to do what I told you!' Donovan growled. He jerked open a cabinet and took out a rifle and a box of bullets. 'Now *move!*'

They called him 'Beef', not because he was a particularly big man, but because his initials were 'B.F,' for Ben Farnham and 'Beef' just seemed to follow when men started calling him 'B-Eff', running the letters together. He was tough, range-hardened, and had worked on Rectangle 5 when Mattie Carr's father had first started the ranch. He had been ramrod for ten years. Now he squinted at Mal Donovan and Reece McCoy as they sat their sweating mounts near the cookfire of the camp and asked about 'Clayton'. Riders were drifting in now that it was getting on towards supper time.

'You're outta luck, Mr Donovan,' Beef told the big scowling rancher. 'The man you're askin' about rode in here all right. I say "rode", but he was barely stayin' in the saddle, reins wrapped around his wrists, tied to the horn. He'd lost a deal of blood from a wound in his side.'

'Well, where the hell is he?' Donovan demanded.

'Oughta be down at the ranch by now. I stitched him up best I could and had Jack Blue run him down in the buckboard. Figured Mattie can look after him better'n me.'

'Goddamnit! That man's a rustler! He was workin' in with Slim Norton – one of *your* men, by the by! Stealin' my mavericks an' puttin' their own brand on 'em.'

Beef scratched at one hairy ear, squinting up at the still mounted rancher. 'Well, we've had our suspicions about Slim but no real proof. You got proof, have you, Mr Donovan?'

'I got all I need! Clayton was s'posed to've been taken into town to the sheriff by Shorty and Tower, but he killed 'em both an' now it looks like he'll get away.'

Beef pursed his lips. 'He ain't goin' far, not beat up like he is. But you want to ride on down to the ranch, Mattie'll likely send someone in for the sheriff, if you want him arrested.'

'You're just "Mr Cooperation", ain't you, Beef?' McCoy growled.

Beef threw him a hard look, unafraid of the man despite his reputation. 'Just bein' neighbourly. A

61

wounded man rides into my camp, I feel duty bound to help him. Still, if it'd been you, McCoy,' Beef shook his head slowly, 'I dunno. Reckon I'd've had to think on it.'

McCoy dropped a hand to his holstered Colt but Donovan snapped, 'Leave it!' He glanced at the sky. 'We oughta make it down to Rectangle before dark.'

'Ain't gonna stop for a cup of java first?' Beef asked innocently. 'Cookie's makin' Son-of-a-Bitch stew, too, and there'd be plenty for you fellers if you want—'

'Piss in your stew!' spat McCoy, wrenching his weary horse's head up. 'I'll settle with you some day, Beef!'

Donovan was already riding, his horse managing to kick over the twin coffee pots at the edge of the cook fire. It earned him a cussing-out by the irate cook but the really inventive epithets were wasted on the Broken D men as they cleared the camp, well out of earshot.

Mattie Carr decided she would have supper first, then check on her patient, before making up her mind whether to send someone to fetch the doctor from town.

This man called Clayton was pretty damn tough, she allowed, rinsing her hands and forearms at the wash-bench outside the ranch kitchen door. He'd been beaten badly; his face was all swollen with bruises and cuts. His own mother would likely have trouble recognizing him. That knife cut was not much more than superficial but it was only by pure luck, the blade had skidded down his ribs, slicing the thin layer of covering flesh. If it had been delivered with just a mite more force the blade would have penetrated some vital organ. He had lost a good deal of blood, but Beef's crude stitching – which must have hurt like hell, having been done with twine and a sacking needle – had been the factor that had slowed the bleeding.

She had tried to make sense of what little Clayton had said; he had passed out with the word *Donovan* slurring from his puffy lips, but it was a tough job.

'Poor devil,' she murmured half-aloud as she dried her hands and arms. 'He's going to be mighty sick and sore when he comes round.'

The land glowed crimson, reflected from the western sky where the long, gunmetal clouds took on colour as the sun died for the night. But as she hung the rag of a towel back on the nail driven into the door frame, she frowned, shading her eyes. There was movement out there, showing in the fiery strip between land and horizon. . . .

It had to be someone from the round-up camp, she figured, coming in from that direction. Yes! She could make out two riders now and although the cook banged the iron triangle, signalling that supper was ready, she stepped up on to the doorstoop, trying to identify the visitors.

Her full lips compressed slightly: *Damnit!* There was only one rider that she knew of who sat so tall in the saddle, and she would consider it a favour of the Good Lord if she never saw him again.

But there was no getting out of this meeting and, resignedly, she stood and waited while her crew settled boisterously on to forms at the long plank table under the dogrun between the ranch kitchen and the bunkhouse.

She watched with slightly accelerating heartbeat as Big Mal Donovan hauled his claybank to a skidding halt and climbed down in that maddening way he had of seeming to take over wherever he set his feet. Reece McCoy she ignored; he wasn't a man you could normally ignore, but she had no time for the mean-eyed gunfighter and made no pretence that she had.

Big Mal touched a hand to his hatbrim and slightly adjusted his dusty eyepatch. ' 'Evenin', Mattie. We've come to collect Clayton.'

'I've always admired your subtle approach, Mal.'

He waved her sarcasm aside. 'Where is he? I'd be obliged if you could have one of your men saddle his horse.'

'Why? He's not going anywhere.'

'That's what you think,' said McCoy flatly.

Mattie didn't even look at him. 'He's lost a lot of blood. He has a large knife wound that's been stitched so he can't be moved. I'm just deciding whether I'll send for Doc Sable – and probably Sheriff Mann.'

Donovan narrowed his one eye, tugged irritably at his moustache, making a short but audible grunting sound.

'The man's been helpin' that hardcase Norton – *your* wrangler – put their brands on my mavericks. Likely some of yours, too. I got no consideration for anyone steals from me.'

'That's interesting, Mal. He told me he's just gotten

back from several years in Mexico, was poisoned by that damn nuisance, Miguel, and had to fight his way past Norton and later your men, Shorty and Tower.'

This wasn't quite true: it had been put together, with a good deal of supposition, by herself and Jack Blue, who had brought Clay down from the round-up camp: Beef had figured most of it from the man's garbled talk while he sewed up the long knife wound and told Blue to pass it on to Mattie.

But she saw by Donovan's face, and the effort he made to close down any expression, that it was close to the truth. 'That's a load of eyewash. He's been workin' with Norton for weeks and I aim to see him end like all rustlers – at the end of a rope.'

She had a full head of henna hair and it whipped across her suntanned face as she shook her head. 'I fibbed, Mal. I've already sent a man to bring out Sheriff Mann.'

Donovan glared and McCoy said, 'Y'ask me, you're *fibbin'* right now!'

'Nobody asked you, McCoy,' she retorted coldly. 'Now, if you want to eat with my men there's plenty of grub to go round. Otherwise I can't see any reason why you don't just ride on back to Broken D before it's full dark.'

A blind man could have seen that Donovan didn't like being spoken to like that. 'You're gettin' just a mite too big for your boots, Mattie. You need to remember you're neighbour to probably the biggest cattle ranch in Texas.'

'Why should that bother me, Mal? I don't have any

ambitions beyond my capabilities.' She even crinkled her pale eyebrows a little, almost smiling. 'And no plans to rework with Saddlebacks.'

Big Mal's mouth tightened and he nearly played his ace in the hole – the money he'd taken from Clayton – but he remained silent. But, damn her! She was a jump ahead of him.

'From what I hear,' he said with a vicious pleasure, 'you ain't got enough cows to make it worthwhile you movin' in there anyway, even if you make your mortgage.'

Mattie's eyes narrowed. 'Oh? Is *that* what you hear?'

The big shoulders shrugged. 'Know your herd-count's way down.'

'Isn't yours?' she countered. His jaw hardened.

'I've lost a lotta mavericks to that damn Norton and his pards! But I can pull through the season right easy, just the same.' There came a crooked smile. 'Can you say that?'

'I can *say* it,' Mattie answered tightly.

Big Mal laughed. 'But it wouldn't be true!'

'Boss, you want, I can drag this Clayton out by the hair,' offered McCoy, hand resting in his gunbutt.

'Well, it would be something to make the sheriff's visit worth while, anyway,' Mattie replied, a tight, challenging smile stretching her full lips.'My complaint, I mean.'

McCoy started forward but Donovan, though steaming, held up a hand, his mean eye stabbing at the girl. 'You got more hide than a Red Angus stud bull, Mattie. That husband of yours knew what he was doin'

66

when he ran out on you.'

'With most of my money!' she snapped, face flushing at Donovan's probing reminder.

Big Mal shrugged. 'Your hard luck. You were mighty . . . subdued, for a time. Now you seem to be gettin' downright . . . obstreperous.'

'Mmmmmm. Yes! I think that's the word, Mal. I feel downright obstreperous. and it feels good.'

McCoy had trouble remaining still and Donovan seemed to be just managing to keep from hitting her.

Then there was a scraping noise as a window just the other side of the kitchen, rose in its slides halfway.

A rifle barrel and a man's shape were visible as a strained voice said, 'Best be – on – your way – Donovan!'

Mattie gasped, outraged 'What're you doing out of bed! You shouldn't—'

'Voices woke me,' Clay Emory grated behind the lace curtain, still sounding as if he could hardly breathe. He was just visible as the rifle barrel jerked. 'You goin', Donovan? I got no love for you and my hands are tired, tremblin'; I wouldn't even have to sneeze to set off the trigger.'

'You ought to be dead by now, Clayton!' Big Mal snapped, turning to his claybank. McCoy headed slowly towards his own mount, looking back at the window. 'Just hold the thought that that oversight'll be taken care of – soon.'

The Broken D men turned their mounts and rode off into the sunset while Mattie ran to the window.

'If that rifle's the one that was on the deer rack in

your room, it's not even loaded.'

She thought she heard Clay give a chuckle. It was followed by the thud of his falling body.

Leaving the ranch, Donovan, in a bad mood, snapped at McCoy who was half-standing in his stirrups, looking back over his shoulder. 'The hell's wrong with you now?'

McCoy ranged his mount alongside his boss, who scowled. 'I think I know that *hombre*, Mal.'

'Clayton?'

McCoy nodded slowly. 'Didn't get a real good look but I'd know that voice anywhere, rough as it was.'

'Well?' demanded the big rancher.

'I *think* his name is Clayton *Emory*. He was a top sergeant when I was in the Army. Heard he made it to a shavetail lieutanant because he busted up a big border slave ring. You know, runnin' young Texas gals down to Mexico City, long after the war, of course, an'—'

'So what? He's a civilian now, ain't he?'

McCoy smiled crookedly. 'That's what I'm wonderin'. Last I heard he'd been transferred to Austin on the strength of breakin' up them slavers. Sent for, they say.'

'What the hell makes that such a big deal?'

'At the time, the Army was recruitin' for a new group they called the Border Rangers, hard men, handy with a gun, who could speak Spanish for undercover work. Later, it became a breakaway unit, separate from the Army. It's growed some since, of course, patrollin' the border. Heard they eventually joined up with the main Texas Rangers.'

'The goddamn Rangers!' Donovan breathed, a step ahead of McCoy. 'I recollect some kinda amalgamation like that a while back. I hope to hell you're wrong, Reece.' He felt a cold sweat drench his big body. 'You know what they say: *One riot – one Ranger. . . .*'

CHAPTER 6

LONG MEMORY

Clay Emory was quite breathless as he hitched his buttocks round to a slightly more comfortable position in the narrow bed. The girl brushed hair out of her eyes, breathing a little faster from having helped him up off the floor.

'It was a courageous but foolish thing to do,' she admonished him. 'You could've broken some of Beef's stitches.'

She took a pair of scissors and cut away the top part of the bandage wrapped around his torso. He bared his teeth but didn't make a sound. 'Oh! You're lucky. Only two broke but the top one's held. I think we can keep the split part closed with some adhesive tape.'

He said nothing, eyes closed now as she worked, his hands clawing at the sheets every so often when it really hurt. She washed away the fresh blood and helped him settle against the pillows, looking closely at his battered face.

'They were very . . . brutal with you.'

He opened his puffy eyes, regarding her in silence before saying, 'I'm obliged for all your help, ma'am, and your trail boss or whoever he is for sewin' me up. But I'll be off your hands quick as I can make myself mend.'

'You'll be "off my hands" as you put it, when I say so!' Her small frown deepened and she looked at him more closely. 'I feel I've seen you somewhere, a long time ago.'

'I don't recall, but you'd better just call me "Clay". Everyone does.'

'All right, and I'm "Mattie". You've had a very rough time of things, Clay. You'll be abed for a week. No more of this foolishness of making out how tough you are, simply because you're a man! You've been beaten and abused, knifed, ridden yourself to near exhaustion, survived a gunfight. You can't expect to spend a night in bed and wake up refreshed and well the next morning.'

'I don't.' He gasped. 'Not now I've come round.'

'Good. You're on my ranch, Rectangle 5, and I'm in charge. You're no trouble, I want you to savvy that! Don't make yourself out to be some kind of martyr, staying in bed because I'm ordering you to. You simply do as I say and we'll both be happy. And you *will* recover your health.'

It was taking its toll, this stiff exchange of words, she could see that, the way he was breathing so raggedly. But she saw the stubbornness on his battered face, too, and felt she was fighting a losing battle.

'All right,' he rasped suddenly, surprising her. 'I admit I feel poorly. I – I'll be happy to stay till I feel better. But I'm the one who'll decide when I leave.'

Mattie heaved a sigh, flapped a hand in exasperation. 'Have it your way.'

She had her hand on the door knob when he said, 'The longer I stay here the more danger you'll be in.'

She snapped her head up, the henna hair swirling. 'Danger?'

'From Donovan. He wants to get his hands on me.' She looked quizzical. 'He's stolen some money from me, a lot of money. The other men who knew about it are dead, though likely McCoy knows. But I guess he's no threat to him.'

'I don't understand. But I do see you're becoming agitated. *No*! Don't argue! I'm bossing you around right now. You get some sleep and we'll talk later. So rest easy.' Then just before she left, she added, 'Mal Donovan and I have been at loggerheads for years.'

He started to reply but suddenly found himself already sliding down into the sleep of near exhaustion.

Sheriff Lucas Mann didn't arrive until the next morning, quite a while after breakfast time. The crew had been sent out to do their work for the day and Mattie met the lawman on the porch.

Mann was just under six feet, heavily built, but the impression it gave was that it was much more muscle than fat. A man about fifty, he had a rugged face, and the corners of the wide mouth tended to droop a little: Lucas Mann rarely smiled. Some grey-streaked hair showed when he doffed his hat and nodded at the ranch woman.

'You know why I'm here, Mattie?'

'I don't *know*, Lucas, but I can guess. Donovan sent you, didn't he?'

'Sent *for* me. I stayed over at Broken D last night. He said you're harbouring a rustler, a man named Clayton. Seems him and your *segundo* Slim Norton were workin' that old racket of burnin' their own brand into any mavericks they found, and they seemed to find a lot belonging to Big Mal.'

'That's Donovan's theory.' Her words were clipped and she made no move to invite the lawman inside. 'I admit we've suspected Slim for some time but we never could catch him at it. Mr Clayton is not his partner. He's just arrived back from Mexico and through no fault of his own was mixed up in some trouble in the hills that involved not only Slim Norton, but that sly Mexican, Miguel Delesandro, and, later Shorty and Tower from Donovan's.'

Mann held up his hand. 'I know the sketchy details. I'm here to question Clayton and get right on down to the nitty-gritty. Now, if you'll let me in, Mattie. . . .'

'You can't see him. He's been badly injured and is still asleep. I – I'm thinking of sending for Doc Sable.'

'Busy man, the doc.' The sheriff eased her aside without much effort. Ignoring her flare of anger he stomped down the short hall and began opening doors.

'Damn you, Lucas!' Mattie stormed after him, pushed him aside and went to a door at the end of the passage. 'He's in here! I resent you storming your way in like this.'

'Sorry,' he muttered unconvincingly, pushing past her. She noticed he had a hand on his holstered Colt as he adjusted his eyes to the gloom, for the shade was pulled down over the window. Mattie, tight-lipped, rolled it up part way and sunlight washed across the bed, showing the lawman the battered Clay Emory.

He was awake, and propped up on several pillows. The facial swelling had gone down considerably and he looked more like his usual self except for dark maps of bruising and a few superficial cuts. His blackened eyes were anxious as he studied the sheriff. Then he seemed to relax a little.

'Checkin' to see if we'd met before, were you?'

'I don't have many friends who are lawmen,' Clay answered raspingly and Mann's lips twitched.

'I'll bet. You know why I'm here.' Mann gestured to the window. 'The porch is only a few feet away. You must've heard me talkin' with Mattie.'

'And what she told you was what happened. I haven't rustled any cattle, Donovan's or anyone else's.'

'Never?'

'Not countin' some cows we took from a bunch of Mexes who'd stole 'em in the first place from a herd I was workin' south of Durango.'

Mann's eyes narrowed. 'Yeah. Heard you'd been in Mexico. What'd you do down there?'

'Sold my share of hosses with Mustang Speers' herd,

74

got robbed and woke up in a rebel camp. I had a choice, ride with 'em or die. . . .' He spread his hands slightly, wincing and leaning quickly towards the left.

'Mind those stitches!' Mattie said sharply.

'I heard different. You were a *mercenario*.' Mann's tone made it clear he did not approve of soldiers of fortune. 'And you were runnin' guns to the rebels. American guns.'

Clay looked concerned now and tried to keep his voice steady as he said, 'Mexico's in one helluva political mess right now, Sheriff. You ride with the wind or get blown outta the saddle.'

'Fill in some details for me. How you got to Mexico, and why, for a start.'

Mattie could see Clayton didn't want to do this and stalled by saying he needed to have the abrasions and bruises on his face bathed and the knife wound dressed. Mann actually smiled this time and spread his hands.

'Whatever you say, Mattie, but while you're gettin' your things ready, Clayton there can explain to me about the guns.' He held up a hand quickly as Clay started to protest. 'You turned over a wagonload of guns to Mex *rebeldes* at a place called La Mirador. Two Mormons caught up in the troubles down there told me, and I got no reason to doubt 'em. But I did some checkin' and it was verified.'

Clay heaved a sigh and nodded. 'Yeah, I did that. But it was in exchange for two families that'd been taken hostage by the rebels.' Mann frowned. 'They knew our wagon train was taking guns to the

Government troops and sent an ultimatum: divert one wagon of the guns to La Mirador or they'd execute the prisoners. I was wagon boss and I made my decision.' Mattie looked horrified and he half-smiled. 'But we removed the firin' pins first on most of 'em. They ever catch up with me, they'll skin me alive. That's why I had to hire Miguel to get me through country I didn't know.'

Mattie looked relieved. Mann said nothing, studying Clay a lot more closely now. The girl brought over a bowl of warm soapy water and some cloths and a towel. She went to work, gently cleaning up Emory's face.

There was some discomfort while she worked on him, but Emory felt a heap better afterwards. Then the girl brushed and combed his hair and he seemed a different man.

The sheriff straightened off the wall, flicked his half-smoked cigarette out of the window, then came over to the bedside and leaned closer to the tensed Emory.

Mattie paused, gathering her bowl of blood-tinged water and her cloths. Her heart beat faster; she could see that Mann had now recognized Clay from somewhere.

The lawman waved a finger near Clay's cleaned-up but still distorted face. 'I – know – you. I ain't quite got it but it'll come. Call yourself Clayton, eh? Well, let's see if I recollect anyone called—' He stopped abruptly, snapped his fingers. 'By Godfrey! Not Clayton just Clay! Clay Emory! There's a fugitive

76

warrant out on you.'

Both men jumped as Mattie dropped the bowl of water. But she ignored its splash and how it swirled across the floor, and stared hard at Emory. Then she stepped closer to the bed, her face very white, hands on her hips. She peered intently at him, her face far from friendly.

'I do believe I recognize you now, too! Clay Emory!' She paused, her nostrils pinched, eyes narrowed and blazing. 'Well, if you are this Emory – and I think you are – I'll thank you for the five thousand dollars you owe me!'

CHAPTER 7

OUT OF THE PAST

It was just over six years ago, when Clay Emory was sheriff of the town of Fremont, south-east of Corrizo Springs on the Nueces River, Dimmit County, Texas: the day the Bellman brothers, Jace and Banjo, arrived and tried to shoot up the entire town.

But Clay recognized it for what it was: a set-up by someone whom Clay had riled by his efforts at law enforcement and who had sent the brothers to put him in Boot Hill. But it had all gone wrong and there had been a foot chase and a violent gunfight in the main street, leaving the Bellmans dead, and also an elderly couple named Carr, who had been just passing through on their way to their home town when their buckboard team had panicked with all the gunfire so close, and overturned the vehicle on to them.

His face bleeding from the bullet crease across his left cheek and breathless from the brief but energetic chase, Clay Emory had just been looking at the obviously deceased old folks lying among the wreckage of the buckboard when a gingham-checkered, henna-haired fury hurtled out of the general store, abused him hysterically and tried to tear his eyes out.

Mattie stiffened as he told this; he was surprised to see the flush in her cheeks as she recalled the incident. 'I – I was upset, *extremely* upset. There were my parents lying dead in the street, all because of your recklessness! We'd only stopped off in town for a meal and to do some shopping on our way home here!' She spoke breathlessly and he saw that the sheriff was mighty interested. 'I thought you were going to kill me, too!'

Clay said, gently. 'I tried to apologize, but – well, your fingernails were aimed squarely at my eyes. Sorry if I got rough.'

'Rough! You almost broke my wrists, the way you flung me to the ground so hard!' Her breasts were heaving as the memories and some of the recollected anger came flooding back.

He continued to stare, then said quietly, 'I was trying to explain how it had happened. You accused me of being trigger happy.'

'I believed you were, and while I may have had doubts over the years in between, I – I'm not so certain now that I wasn't right all along, with all those dead men you've left behind you.' She gestured vaguely towards the unseen mountains. 'What else can I think?'

'Yeah. Well, trouble seems to follow me around.

Like you suing for that compensation.'

'It wasn't my idea!' she snapped, her eyes beginning to glisten. 'I was just a young woman, not even out of my teens and – and you took my parents from me!'

Lucas Mann was watching and listening with unabashed interest, flicking his gaze from one to the other, not interrupting, preferring to let them give him the story in angry bursts; that way you got more details, he reckoned.

'As I recall, you had someone else lookin' out for you,' Clay said quietly, and he saw her frown and flush again.

Her mouth tightened, her face became pale and taut. 'You must mean my fiancé, of course. Dalton Banks.'

'Don't recall the name, but I thought he was your husband.'

There was a long silence, broken only by the sounds of the hard breathing of the woman and Emory, whose emotions of that day in Fremont came surging back vividly. Surprisingly, when Mattie spoke her voice was much calmer. 'Dalton was a fortune hunter. I was too young and naïve to see it then. I was flattered by his attentions; he claimed a very good background, with parents back East. Said they owned a string of department stores in Chicago. It was all lies to impress my father; he had his sights set on our ranch and he saw marriage to me as a way of getting it.' She shuddered a little. 'I was a silly little fool! Ran off with him and got married, even before my father had investigated his claims properly. Then there was the buckboard crash.'

She stopped speaking briefly. 'Dalton said he was sure the County could be sued because you were one of its employees and I was entitled to compensation because of your negligence, not taking due care, or something like that—'

'And he was right,' cut in Sheriff Mann. 'I take it you agreed to this Banks handling the proceedings?'

She used her apron irritably to wipe the tears away now. 'I – I really don't know. Oh, he was a – a despicable man! He took advantage of my grief and being so naïve. I was very young, you know, I knew little about the world and worried mightily about trying to run the Rectangle; it was a big responsibility. Luckily the ranch was in my name, thanks to Dad's will. But Dalton was now legally my husband and, well, you men being unfairly considered as much more *responsible* than us females, he went ahead with the compensation claim, and eventually the money was paid over to him. Seven thousand five hundred dollars. Which was a lot at that time.'

'It ain't hay even now,' allowed the sheriff.

'Dalton gave me five hundred dollars, paid the shyster lawyers he'd employed another two thousand and – and disappeared with the rest. He also tried to sell the ranch but I – I was stubborn and wouldn't sign an authority for that.'

Silence was heavy in that sunlit stuffy ranch room for a few minutes until Clay asked curtly: 'So how come you figure *I* owe you five thousand?'

She wouldn't look at him, lowered her gaze and shook her head several times. 'I – I'm sorry. I didn't mean that. God knows I didn't want money obtained that way in the first place, but. . . .' She sighed. 'Over the years I've had such a battle running the ranch. Somehow I managed to keep it out of Dalton's hands and many a time, when I felt despair, I did think about all that money.'

'And me, it seems.'

She looked as if she might break out into a full-blown crying jag but managed to keep control. 'I said I was sorry! And I'm thoroughly ashamed of trying to claw your eyes. It was a – a terrible thing to do. I apologize.'

He saw how upset she was and merely shrugged, wincing as sharp pain ran down the line of sutures in his wound. 'I thought you still used your married name?'

'I – I could never find Dalton to file for a divorce. I have no idea where he is, so . . . I'm stuck with it.'

'A rat like that likely has a dozen different names, Mattie,' Mann said gruffly. ' "Banks" mightn't even be his real name. You may not even be legally married to him. I was you, I'd keep usin' your original name of Carr. It's a sad story, but there's still that fugitive warrant out on Emory there.' He looked coldly at the injured man. 'And strangely enough, it's because you ran out on paying any compensation to Mattie.'

'But – but I – I never filed such a complaint!' she breathed. 'I knew Dalton was considering it but I was too upset and trying to learn to run the ranch. I didn't really know what he was about. I may've told him to go ahead. I don't think I even cared very much at that time. I had worries enough.'

'He likely fixed the warrant on the quiet. Just in case Emory came up with a challenge that might've delayed payment of the money. He figured that Emory would run when he found out he was being stuck for five thousand dollars.'

'That wasn't why I went to Mexico,' rapped Clay, an edge of anger in his voice.

'That's what it said on the warrant. "Absconding from legal debt".'

'Don't care what it said. At the time I never knew about the compensation. I knew Banks had started some sort of legal action over the death of Mattie's folks but I'd quit Fremont by then, fired by the County. I figured it was their problem anyway.'

'So you crossed the Rio,' Mann said, very serious now. 'If it wasn't anything to do with the money, why?'

Emory gave him a hard, steady stare. 'It's nothing to do with you, Mann. Nor Mattie.'

'Well, I tell you right now, Emory, it damn well does have somethin' to do with me! In my capacity as sheriff of this here town of Turnabout Creek, I'm duty bound to enforce any active warrants in my possession. I aim to find out what it is. And you'll damn well stay in my jail until I do! Hurt or no.'

The cell was large enough to take a dozen Saturday night drunks with a little squeeze here and there, but Clay Emory had it all to himself.

He sat up on a hard bunk, using the thin pillow Mann had given him to keep his back off the wall, smoking. Nothing he said could change Mann's mind about keeping him locked up. He'd raised what hell he could, but had to pull his horns in before the sheriff became too suspicious. As it was, Clay was sure Mann figured he was a professional gun-runner, had used the cover of sheriff of Fremont to ship guns to the Mexican rebels.

'It's an offence punishable by death or life in prison, Emory,' Mann pointed out. 'But you give me some useful information and I'll see it works in your favour.'

'You mean I should trust you?' Clay said scornfully. and the lawman's eyes narrowed, his jaw hardening.

'I hold your life in my hands, you damn fool!'

'The hell're you making all these threats to me for anyway? Life imprisonment, death penalty. I'm no gun-runner.'

'Facts say different.'

'What "facts"?'

Mann started to move away from the bars. 'Ones you're holding back. But I've got better things to do than stand here wastin' my breath on you. I'm a workin' lawman, which means I got law to enforce, and I aim to do just that.'

As he was going through the door leading to the passage, Clay said quietly, 'Long as Big Mal says it's OK, huh?'

Lucas Mann stopped dead in his tracks, spun on his heels and Clay stiffened when he saw the cocked six-gun in his hand. Hell! That had been a mighty fast draw!

Mann approached the bars again, still pointing the gun, giving his prisoner a mighty cold glare. Then he slowly lowered the hammer and holstered the Colt, though he kept his hand on the butt. He took a deep breath.

'I am not Donovan's man, Emory. I took an oath to enforce the County and State laws, and that's what I aim to do. Anyone who thinks different better keep such thoughts to himself. You savvy?'

Clay said nothing but slowly relaxed.

After another hard stare the sheriff left the cell block area and Emory released a long slow breath he hadn't been conscious of holding.

Seems he could've made a mistake about Lucas Mann. . . . Well, mebbe.

Mattie, contrite and wanting to make a few things up to Clay Emory, to salve her own conscience, he reckoned bitterly, brought in Doctor Sable to check him over.

The doctor was middle-aged, efficient enough, going by frontier standards of the day, very terse and in a hurry.

'You're a tough man, sir. You have good powers of recuperation, and I see by your many scars that you have had plenty of practice.'

Emory ignored that part and said, 'How long before I'm up and about, Doc?'

'I have no doubt your body will tell you that – or, if you are as butt-headed as I suspect, you will make the decision, regardless.' The medic snapped his bag closed, paused at the cell door where Lucas Mann waited, one hand on his gun. 'The knife wound is not all that serious. The blade skidded over the ribs and while those sutures will certainly aid healing, they really weren't necessary. At the same time, you shouldn't attempt to break in any mustangs or get into any brawls. You understand me? Good day to you. I'll leave your bill with the sheriff.'

He bustled out, Mann and Mattie following, and Clay adjusted his clothes, waited impatiently for the lawman to return. When he reappeared, Clay said,

'You still gonna hold me here?'

'You haven't told me your reasons for crossing the border yet.'

'What the hell's it matter? I'm back, ain't I?'

'You certainly are! Leaving five men dead along the way! In my county.'

'You weren't around for me to ask permission to shoot 'em.'

Mann almost smiled. 'No. And there's not even a small chance I'd've given you that permission, anyway. But I want a written statement from you – in full.'

'What's your game, Sheriff? You know damn well you don't need to hold me.'

'Don't know that at all. You haven't even begun to convince me you weren't runnin' guns.'

Clay chewed briefly at his lower lip, studying the lawman closely. 'Would you send a telegraph message for me?'

'Mebbe, if you pay for it.'

Clay made an exasperrated sound, knuckles white where his hands gripped the bars. 'All right. Gimme a pencil and paper and I'll write out what I want to say.'

When Clay had printed his message and handed the paper back through the bars, Lucas Mann read quickly, lips moving a little with the words, then looked up quickly.

'This some kinda code? "*Accomodation not to my liking*", and here "*Need funds or help*". And who's this "Counsellor Worth" in San Antone you've addressed it to? You figurin' on gettin' a lawyer at this late stage?'

'Just send it, Sheriff. OK?'

For a moment it seemed that Mann might tear up the paper, but he turned slowly and walked off down the dimly lit passage, still studying the written words. 'After I have your statement and it satisfies me, I'll give it some consideration.'

'Dammit! All right, get me some more paper and I'll give you your damn statement. I'll need a box or something to lean on while I write it.'

The sheriff hesitated, then reached down the ring of keys from the wall peg, drawing his six-gun with his other hand. 'OK. You can come through to my office and write it up. But I'll be holding this gun on you all the time, so don't get any ideas of trying to make a run for it.'

Clay looked at him coldly as the sheriff slid the key into the lock. The lawman returned his gaze. 'I mean it. I'll shoot you down you try to escape, Emory.'

Clay was convinced the man was serious and held his hands shoulder high while the door was opened and Mann, prodding him in the back with his Colt, marched him through to the front office where a lamp, turned low, burned dully.

Fact was, Clay was breathing heavily when he reached it and was glad to drop into the indicated desk chair; he wasn't as fit as he'd figured, but he did his best to hide it from the lawman.

'Top drawer there's some writin' paper. Pen and ink you can see on the desk.' Mann sat down across from Clay and watched his every move very closely. 'No, don't turn up the lamp, dammit! We're almost out of oil and the general store can't get delivery for another couple of days.'

'A man could go blind,' grumbled Clay as he dipped the pen in the stone inkwell, then began to write, hunching close to the paper in the bad light.

He had only scrawled a few words when the first shot shattered the side window and the lamp exploded, hurling broken glass and splashes of hot oil across the scattered papers.

Emory dived beneath the desk and Mann leapt up, shooting at the window. A gun flashed there, twice, and Clay heard the sheriff gasp and then fall to the floor, not two feet from where he crouched in the desk well.

Without conscious thought, Clay snatched the Colt from the groaning sheriff, kicked over the chair behind him and spun round, shooting at the window as the killer's gun there blazed in a series of fast shots. Wood splintered above him, a sliver stinging his neck. The gun flashes briefly showed a narrow face beneath a battered hat. The man reared back as Clay's bullets ripped up the window frame. No doubt broken glass and splintered wood took the killer in the face, as he lurched away, grunting.

Clay clambered to his feet, feeling the burning pain of his knife wound as the crude stitches sawed through his flesh. He ran to the window, flattened against the wall, looked out briefly, his chest heaving with the effort.

Something or someone moved in the darkness of the alley and he triggered again. He wasn't sure but he thought the man staggered. Then he turned back into the office, hearing Mann sob in agony as he tried to pull himself upright by the front of the scarred desk.

In the dark, Clay felt the Colt cylinder: one bullet left. 'Where you hit?'

'I'll – manage – but you gimme – that – gun,' grated Mann, reaching out one hand. There was blood on the back of it and the shirtsleeve was soggy.

Clay shook his head and started to sidle around towards the door, his Colt covering the lawman. 'One bullet left, Mann. You try to stop me and you're dead.'

'S-so're – you if you go out that door.'

'I don't think so,' Clay said as the sheriff grunted and sprawled across the desk before rolling off to the floor.

Outside he heard people shouting and running feet. He groped his way to the wall where he remembered seeing a rifle on a bracket; his own gunbelt hung from the same peg.

'There're people outside, Mann. Do some yellin'. You're pretty good at that. Someone'll get the sawbones for you.'

89

'You – bust out – and you'll need – an – under-taker!'

'Well, kinda drastic, I guess but I could use a litte peace and quiet. *Adios*, Sheriff.'

Opening the rear door, he paused. 'Oh – don't bother with that telegram now. I got all the help I need.'

He brandished the rifle and went out into the night as someone tentatively opened the street door and called Mann's name into the darkness of the office.

If Mann made any sound it was drowned out by the slamming of the rear office door.

CHAPTER 8

FUGITIVE

'How the *hell* could you make such a damn stupid mistake!'

Big Mal Donovan didn't, for once, roar the question at the top of his voice, but spoke quietly though with a heavy, bitter edge to his words.

He glared across the table at McCoy, who was seated in a straightback chair holding a wet rag to his face, which was pocked with small cuts and two ragged gashes where slivers of wood had been painfully removed. He knew he was lucky he hadn't been blinded by the flying glass from the law office window when Emory had fired at him.

His free hand shook as he reached for the bottle of the Demon but the big rancher snatched it out of reach.

'Christ, Mal! I – I need a good shot of that! I coulda been blinded, you know.'

'Then you'd have a real excuse for mistaking Mann for Clay Emory,' the rancher told him callously. 'I'm waitin' for you tell me how come!'

Feeling sick and hard done by, McCoy sighed. 'Mann had the damn lamp turned right down because of the general shortage of oil, I guess. But he was sittin' in the visitor's chair and Emory was behind the desk. With all that shadow, them bein' roughly the same size, I aimed at the wrong one. I'm sorry, Mal. Can I have a shot of the Demon now?'

For a moment he thought the rancher was going to refuse, but then that single eye, cold as a bullet rattling around in a bloody kidney dish, blinked and the bottle was thrust into McCoy's groping hand. The gunfighter drank and gasped, took a second swallow and bent over double, coughing.

His eyes were streaming when he straightened. His voice was almost falsetto as he said, 'Needed that!'

'What you need is my size fourteen boot buried in your ass! Goddammit, Mac, it was served to you on a platter and you still. . . . Aaah! The hell with it! What we've got to come to terms with now is that Clay Emory's on the loose and if he's who I think he is, we're in a helluva lot of trouble. Unless he's stopped – dead!'

'I'll get some of the boys in the mornin' and we'll comb these hills so good a flea can't get through.'

Donovan's eye glittered. 'That's a good idea, except not in the mornin' – do it now! Pick five men and you be on Emory's trail within an hour.'

McCoy moaned, started to reach for the bottle

again, but changed his mind. He lurched to his feet, muttering, 'Mann's likely got a posse out already. He weren't hit all that bad!'

Receiving no reply, he stumbled towards the doorway under Donovan's unwavering stare.

The big rancher sat there pressing his thick finger-tips together for a few minutes, the lone eye wavering towards the bottle of Demon. But he made no move to take a drink, stood abruptly, the chair toppling but ignored as he crossed the room to a wall map.

He grabbed the desk lamp – not turned low, this one: Broken D had a plentiful supply of coal oil. He held it close to the lower left-hand corner. Part of the map edge had curled up where it had been torn away from the thumbtack holding it to the timber. Donovan straightened the offending piece and matched it up to the body of the map. He peered closely, holding the lamp close, running a finger in a shallow horseshoe movement, following the line of a marked creek and coming to rest on the paper's edge, where the map ended.

It was named Turnabout Creek. He scratched his jaw as he studied the rugged country within the waver-ing arms of that creek before it met the Rio Grande. One arm ran along a line of hills that were the outer boundary of Broken D. On the far side of the hills was land belonging to Rectangle 5.

'Goddam!' he breathed, slapping the back of his knuckles hard on the area. The thick map paper made a cracking sound, like a muted gunshot. 'Worst deci-sion I ever made sellin' that land off to Jonas Carr!'

The words naming the area were simple:
The Saddlebacks.

The round-up camp was in almost total darkness when Clay Emory dismounted within the tree line, far enough out for the heavy, measured panting of his hard-ridden mount not to wake the sleeping Rectangle crew. They were scattered untidily around the low-burning campfire, but he saw that two wagons each had a man sleeping beneath them. One was the chuckwagon, so that would be the cook snoring there.

The other was a gear wagon and he figured the man in those blankets underneath would be Beef, the camp boss.

He patted the sweating horse, let the reins trail; he hoped it knew enough to just graze a small area and didn't wander off. He had taken it from the stables behind the law office and knew Mann was vindictive enough to add its theft to the charges already against him. He was wearing his gunbelt, carrying his own Winchester, limping as he moved closer to the bedroll that he figured contained the sleeping Beef.

He was right – except Beef wasn't asleep and Emory jumped hard enough to bring a gasp of pain from him as stiff muscles jarred down his left side. He froze as a dark form rose quickly away from the blanket and rolled out from beneath the wagon.

Starlight and some reflected glow from the banked campfire glinted briefly from the cocked pistol in the Rectangle man's hand.

'What the hell d'you want, sneakin' up like this!'

Clay held the rifle out from his side lifted his free hand shoulder high. 'Take it easy, Beef! It's me, Clayton. Recollect you sewed me up?'

'I know who you are. My question still stands.' Then he leaned forward a little and swore. 'Hell! You ain't got *another* wound for me to tend!'

Clay briefly touched the blood smearing the back of his left hand and shook his head. 'Came close, but only burned across my upper arm. It's just leakin' a mite. McCoy did it.'

By now other rannies were stirring and he heard leather creak as a couple unsheathed their weapons and cocked hammers. Beef called softly: 'Get your rest, you men. We've got that big round-up tomorrer. *Get your rest*, I said! I'll handle this – whatever it is.'

He stepped forward as Clay staggered a little, reached out and grabbed the sideboard of the wagon. Beef hesitated, then holstered his Colt and steadied the wounded man, easing him to the ground.

'You enjoy bein' a target?'

Emory gave him a crooked smile. 'Not really. Wound's nothin'. I'm just plumb tuckered.'

The cook was awake now and Beef said to bring some hot water and a cloth. What the cook said does not bear repeating – and likely wouldn't see the light of day in print, anyway. But he moved to obey and within minutes, Beef had ripped Emory's shirtsleeve shoulder high, washed the bullet burn, and tied a narrow strip of flourbag around it.

'Oughta hold you.' Clay had told Beef what had happened while the man worked on his arm. 'You

95

sound like one of them poor bastards has a devil ridin' his shoulder, so that no matter where he goes or what he does, trouble's only a breath away.'

Clay nodded solemnly as Beef placed a newly rolled cigarette between his lips. The ramrod quickly rolled one for himself and lit both, squatting beside Clay who now sat with his back against a wagon wheel.

When they had smoked about half their cigarettes, Beef said quietly, 'You're kinda lost, ain't you?'

Clay looked at him sharply, half-smiled again and nodded. 'In more ways than one, I guess.'

'You on the dodge?' Beef knew a man took a chance asking another if he was running from the law and expected to walk away with all his teeth. But this close to the border anyone in a situation like Clay Emory just had be running from something – or someone.

But Clay made no hostile movements: he was too damn tired and plumb wore out anyway. 'There are a few Mexes'd like to get their hands on me. Some gringos, too, apart from Lucas Mann and Donovan.'

Beef nodded. 'Had me an idea Big Mal was in it someplace. The man's so damn arrogant I reckon he'd spit in the Governor's eye if he took the notion. Old enemies, huh?'

'No. Never set eyes on him till a couple days ago. Heard plenty, of course; never knew what to believe and what was just trail talk.'

'Believe whatever you hear. There's likely some truth in it somewheres.' Beef was quiet a moment and added, 'You gonna tell me why you come to my camp?'

Clay nodded slowly. 'I guess I figure you for a man

who don't deal in much gossip, Beef. But I need to find out a few things about Mattie Carr, as well as Donovan.'

The mention of Mattie's name stiffened Beef's shoulders and with the sudden, deep draw on his cigarette, the glow showed narrowed eyes amongst all those wrinkles.

'You wanna turn in and catch a little sleep; you could be gone before sunup. Then I wouldn't have to kill you. I'll even tell you a way outta these hills.'

Clay nodded slowly. 'About what I expected you to say, but I don't wanta know nothing bad about her, even if there is anythin', Beef. Donovan, sure, the more I know about how mean the sonuver is the better. But Mattie – well – I better tell you now, was me got her folks killed in Fremont six years ago.'

Half the crew had their ears hanging out by now, of course, and Beef sat there silently while Emory related the story of his gunfight with the Hellman brothers.

When he had finished Beef flicked his cigarette away and looked steadily into Clay's face. 'She know it was you?'

'Yeah. Not when she first doctored me, but a while afterwards the subject came up.'

'An' she never kicked you off Rectangle?'

'Hell, no! But I thought she was gonna rip Mann's ears off when he insisted on throwin' me in his jail.'

Beef sighed. 'Yeah, that'd be Mattie; about a third the size of Donovan, but with a heart three times bigger. Which ain't always a good thing.' His stare intensified and he paused, obviously waiting for

Emory to add something to his story.

Clay poked a dead twig into the ground between his scuffed and filthy boots, then looked squarely at Beef. 'Would you take my word that I won't intentionally cause Mattie any hurt? I . . . well, some things I gotta do are a mite . . . delicate, but I'll do my best to walk all around Mattie and Rectangle 5. I can't say more right now, Beef.'

He let the words hang and Beef's expression didn't change. 'Not quite sure what you're gettin' at, but if it's what I think. . . . Look, long ago, I swore to Mattie's father I'd look out for her – always. This was right after the trouble with that bastard Banks, marryin' her and then runnin' off, an' Donovan stirrin' the pot just for good measure. My word still holds an' you'll have to do a helluva lot to persuade me to tell you even one more thing about Mattie.'

He stood abruptly, hooked a thumb in his gunbelt close to the Colt's butt.

'You be gone by sunup. Cooky'll give you a sack of grub and I'll throw in a box of bullets. But when the mornin' fire etches the Saddlebacks, you be missin', feller.'

'I'd like to get a decent sleep here, Beef. Mebbe I'm more poorly than I figured,' Clay said somewhat feebly.

'You'll be a mighty lot poorer if you let it keep you here past my deadline. All right, Cooky, fix him up. You rannies get back in your bedrolls. Show's over an' you got lotsa chores to look forward to. While you watch Clayton here ride off into the sunrise.' He swung his hard gaze to Clay. 'Savvy?'

Emory sighed. 'All too well, Beef. All too well.'

Beef spat. 'Then you might be a leetle smarter than I gave you credit for. Don't prove me wrong.'

Then he dropped to one knee and began rearranging his rumpled bedroll. Cooky brought the grubsack and a canteen, dropped them beside Clay where he was slumped against the wagon wheel, but only for a couple of minutes more. Then he climbed slowly to his feet, picked up his rifle, canteen, and grubsack, and walked slowly towards where he had left the stolen horse.

As he rode off, he saw a glint of metal poking between the spokes of the wagon wheel beside the spot where Beef had spread his blankets. The gun barrel followed him until the darkness swallowed him. He smiled grimly.

Now he was in strange country, alone, and a fugitive – not to mention being only about fifty per cent fit. And that was being mighty optimistic.

Coming here had been a bad idea – real bad!

He had the uncomfortable feeling that it could only get worse.

CHAPTER 9

THE SADDLEBACKS

Sometime before there was more than just a smeary band of grey blanching the eastern sky, he fell out of the saddle on a high trail.

The horse, a big-chested bay, gave a small whinny and shied to one side as Clay's body skidded off the trail and slid down the slope beyond. The impact and continuing movement brought him out of the semi-comatose state he had been in: a kind of self-hypnosis he used when he was forced to ride even though wounded and in need of rest. It had saved his life several times in the past.

Pain was a living, writhing thing in his battered body, and his aching hands groped wildly for some means of stopping his tumbling descent. Suddenly, a slim sapling almost stove in his ribs, and even as the breath gusted out of him he managed to hook the crook of his right arm around the sapling's trunk. It felt like the arm was tearing loose in its socket and his head sank down, lights whirling behind his eyes. Scrabbling instinctively, his boots at last found purchase enough to halt all movement.

Gasping, he began to pull himself up closer to the sapling, but decided the effort was too much. Or maybe it was just that the air was thinner here; for somehow he had hit a very steep section of range and, rather than turn back, he'd figured high ground was always an advantage. It usually was.

But not if a man couldn't stay on his horse.

He sagged against the tree as he closed his eyes and plunged into darkness.

When he awoke, the sun was warm, and bright enough for him to have to lift one hand between it and his eyes, though he still had to squint.

He was disoriented, but only for a few moments; the aches and pains and the welcoming whinny of the bay grazing on a patch of nearby grass brought the memories rushing in.

Five minutes later, after a lot of grunting effort, he managed to drag himself to the upper side of the sapling. He flopped with his back against the trunk, no longer having to worry about sliding down the steep slope. The horse came over to nudge him and he managed to grab a stirrup and pull himself upright so he could unhook the canteen and the grubsack. Legs awobble, he fumbled in the saddle-bags and found a small bag of grain he'd hoped would be there; Lucas Mann had struck him as the kind of man who would look after any horse he rode. He shook some grain into his cupped hand.

After another ten minutes, the hunger of both man and animal satisfied, Clay punched in the crown of his hat, spilled a cupful of water into it and gave it to the bay.

When he sat down again, his back sliding down the sapling's trunk, he checked there was a cartridge in the rifle's breech and sat there, listening to the birds fluttering about their business in the trees on the slope, calling sweetly, sometimes harshly, never still, full of life. A reassuring sound to a man unsound in body.

After a while he also detected the trickle of water somewhere close by. It startled him as it finally impinged itself upon his drifting consciousness and he sat half-upright. It was coming from below, far below. When he hitched around stiffly, he could see the creek glinting through the foliage. It seemed to flow towards the distant Rio, so it had to be Turnabout Creek.

'Seems I'm not as lost as I figured.' His voice sounded strange against the background of the birds and the running water and the rising breeze rustling the leaves. It was like an intrusion, foreign to this isolated area.

But not as foreign as gunfire!

A brief, ragged volley of shots came from well below his position, briefly drowned the musical sounds of the water. The birds stopped their sweet callings and chattering and wings whumped as they flew away to a safe distance: hear a sound, get well out of reach before stopping to decide whether it was safe or otherwise. Good idea, but he had nowhere to run to. He listened as the gun's echoes slapped away, followed by a distant sound that could only be produced by a human voice.

A man was calling, his brief words followed by a strange ululating sound that cowboys use, mostly on round-up, to hurry up a lazy bunch of cattle. Or to call them in closer. Drag riders often fired off a few shots like he had just heard, to hasten any stragglers along: familiar round-up sounds, these. But way out here? This far past the boundaries of any of the ranches?

'Not usual, *amigo!*' he told himself, struggling to get the rifle around into a more accessible position.

He squinted against the glare, straining to see through the timber, cursing the creek's sparkle through the leaves. Just as he was about to give up the calling and odd gunshots started up again, but drifting away. Lifting slightly, he saw dust lazily curling across the lower slopes.

And now he could hear the bawling of cattle: a lot of cattle.

Queer, when this area was so far from the range used by Broken D or Rectangle 5. He knew that much from having scanned the wall map back in Donovan's office – without making it obvious he was studying it.

One answer was rustlers, driving stolen beef towards the Rio, where they could swim them across into Mexico.

He took another long swallow of water, stuffed some dry though reasonably fresh biscuits into his mouth and stiffly mounted the bay. He checked his six-gun, laid the loaded Winchester across his thighs and set the horse moving downslope, weaving slowly and confidently through the trees.

There were six riders; two, maybe three, he recognized as men he had seen while on Broken D. The others could be Donovan men, too, for all he knew, but they were strangers to him, and there was at least one Mexican *vaquero*.

Whoever they were, they knew their business as they drove the bunch of at least sixty cows along the lower arm of the roughly horseshoe-shaped creek. Clay knew from Donovan's wall map that the upper arm of the creek started at the north-western edge of the Saddlebacks country, flowing in from the Rio for a couple of miles before swinging abruptly towards the east for another mile, then looping once more, roughly parallel to the upper arm, feeding back into the lower reaches of the big river.

There was a rugged, short though steep range of hills between the creek's arms – where he was now, he figured – that prevented a clear view of the creek's entire upper confluence with the Rio Grande. With other lumpy rises of land, mostly heavily timbered, it was difficult to see that Turnabout Creek had two arms unless, like Clay Emory, a man was high enough up.

That was why it was a perfect place for rustlers to bring their stolen stock: both sections of the creek could not be seen at the same time from ground level. Which made it easy to load the cattle from the lower arm of the creek, on to waiting riverboats making unscheduled and unrecorded stops on their way south-east towards the Gulf, with many opportunities to unload their illegal cargoes along the way, almost all on the Mexican side.

As he figured this, his head still throbbing, though benefiting from whatever little rest he had been able to snatch, another thought occurred to him.

If it worked with rustled cattle – and it would – then it would work just as well – or better – with guns.

There was a kind of bluff, a collection of huge boulders, a couple with large bushes dotted over their northern edges blocking his view of the big river.

But even as he sniffed wood smoke he saw the drifting dark smudge rising beyond the boulders, broken a little by a weak breeze. There would be a boat anchored down there, just inside the creek where it would be deepest at the point where it joined the Rio: Manzano Point, already waiting to take the cattle on board.

So, his theory was right. By the volume of smoke that was smearing the blue sky he figured the steam pressure was up, the giant paddle wheels ready to churn as soon as the cows were on board.

He'd seen such an operation once before, a few years ago. It was well upriver, off the mostly uninhabited strip between Piedras Negras and the northern section of Webb County. At that time a Mexican traitor, eager for the Yankee dollars ready to be paid for genuine information leading to the whereabouts of the *rebelde* masses, had given the game away. Unfortunately for him, the chief ranger had insisted he accompany the squad to where he claimed the rendezvous would take place before any reward was paid. But the *revolucionarios* were more alert than the traitor had figured, and he was the first to die: shot out of the saddle by one of the men he had betrayed.

It had been a brief, intense fight and the riverboat, in its hurry to escape, had left half the cattle swimming in the river then promptly run up on a sandbank, the paddle wheel shattering. It was still regarded as one of the most successful actions of the New Border Patrol, and the first time the Mexican and US authorities had fully cooperated.

Good memories, *amigo*, Clay told himself, but there are no heavily armed troops here to back you up; you're on your own.

What chance did a lone man have against that bunch below? Not to mention an unknown number of bearded, wild-eyed Mexicans waiting on the riverboats: representatives of the rebels, hungry for beef and eager to spill the blood of any interfering fool of a gringo.

He knew the answer to that one without having to struggle to think about it. But. . . .

Mal Donovan yanked open the door of the small cubbyhole built on to the main bunkhouse and yelled at the dark figure curled up on the bunk.

'McCoy, you lazy bastard! Get outta that bunk before I throw you over the goddam barn!'

106

Reece McCoy started and sat up before he knew what he was doing. He blinked in the early sunlight that outlined the huge figure stooping in the doorway.

'Wh . . . what? Aw, hell, Mal! I only just got to sleep! Been out all night tryin to track that Clayton son of a bitch.'

'Well, did you get him?' Donovan didn't give the half-awake man time to answer. 'No! You did not! And I told you, don't come back without him! Preferably his corpse but—'

'Jesus Christ, Mal! Have a heart, dammit!' McCoy snarled, fatigue and the thunder of Big Mal's voice booming around the small room making his throbbing head sound like a whole bunch of war drums inside his skull. 'Will you get off my back! You're runnin' me into the ground. I'm no damn good to you, myself or anyone else like this! I need a decent sleep. Just an hour or two without you bawlin' me out. If I don't get it, I'm quittin'. I mean it, Mal! I've had a bellyful of this endless cussin' me for no useful purpose. Now what's it to be?'

Donovan's face seemed mostly blank as the sun was behind him, but through his anger McCoy thought he saw a wave of shock wash over those big, coarse features. Truth be known, his own heart was beating like the war drums in his head and his belly was all knotted up at his temerity.

But he was at the end of his tether and he knew damn well he *would* quit if Donovan didn't back off. At the same time he wondered whether he would live long enough to have to make the decision.

107

'Hell almighty! You must have a hangover like a whole slew of Saturday nights catchin' up with you.' Donovan spoke harshly but there was a rising edge of surprise in his voice and he even paused to clear his throat. 'OK. Mebbe I've been pushin' too hard. You can have your hour's sleep, I'll even give you two. But I'll damn well expect results! Take that thought with you when you hit the pillow!'

The door slammed, rattling in its frame, and McCoy blinked, lay back with a half-smile forming on his beard-shagged face. But he wasn't surprised to find his brow damp with sweat when he ran the back of a hand over it.

Then he lay down and pulled the blanket over his head.

Of course, he never did get his two hours' promised sleep; he was too worked up and worried about the consequences of his outburst for that.

Grumbling, head aching above his eyes, he washed up at the bench and argued with the cook about a hot breakfast. Afterwards he went across to Donovan's office where the big man was sitting behind his desk, smoking a pipe.

'The walkin' dead,' was the greeting that stopped McCoy just inside the door. 'While you been snorin' your head off, Ringo rode in to say halfway through loadin' the cows on to the boats, someone up on the ridge started pot-shottin' at 'em. Knocked two men outta the saddles, kept shootin' at the boat crew as soon as they tried to slide the planks out for the cows to walk up, even dropped a few cows, blockin' the trail in.'

'Aw, Judas Priest! Don't tell me it's that goddam Clayton!'

'Ringo saw him. It's him, all right, and he's got the high ground. Now you get up there and—'

'I know, I know. Bring you his corpse!'

Donovan took the pipe from his mouth, eyes narrowed.

'Or don't bother comin' back.'

Reece McCoy grunted; he turned to leave, stopped, then looked back over his shoulder, smiling crookedly.

'Here's somethin' to make your day. Sheriff Mann's just dismountin' by the corrals.'

Mal Donovan gripped his pipe so hard the stem snapped.

Lucas Mann had his left arm in a sling and there was a square patch of plaster at the base of his neck on the right-hand side. His face was drawn with pain lines as he dropped into the chair across the desk from Donovan. McCoy was standing by the door, figuring he'd better stay. Big Mal's gaze was on the lawman.

'You look kinda poorly, Lucas.'

'Feel it, too. Look, Mal, no time to beat about the bush. Clayton stole my horse, the bay, and I've been ridin' a jughead from the livery. It's one the livery hires out for folk to ride in the foothills Sunday afternoons. Got no stamina. Like to borrow one of your mounts, somethin' with stayin'-power.'

'You can *hire* one.' Donovan smiled thinly. 'Figure you'll be payin' with County money.'

'All right, all right,' Mann said irritably. 'Be too much to ask if any of your men've seen Clayton, I guess?'

109

McCoy opened his mouth to deny it but let his jaw hang as Donovan said, 'Matter of fact Ringo, one of my outriders, came in not long ago. Said this Clayton turned up outta nowhere an' took a couple shots at him.'

'The hell you say! Man's trigger-happy, all right. Damn, I was gonna grab some breakfast before movin' on but I better start now. Where'd he jump Ringo?'

'Over towards the Saddlebacks.'

Mann nodded slowly. 'Made good time. I tell you that bay's a damn fine horse, and I want it back. The Saddlebacks huh? I'll be mighty hungry before I get that far.'

'Cooky'll give you somethin'. Mac, you fix it and saddle the big Appaloosa for Lucas. An' ride with the sheriff. You know all the short cuts to the Saddlebacks.'

'Yeah, sure.' McCoy left but not before throwing Donovan a frown.

Twenty minutes later he was standing on the stoop outside Big Mal's office while Mann, after a good breakfast, was using the privy.

'Why the hell you sendin' me to nursemaid Mann?'

Donovan smiled thinly, but before he could speak the puzzled gunfighter added, 'And sendin' him to the Saddlebacks! If Ringo's tryin to load them rustled steers on to the boats—'

'Don't matter. Mann's never gonna tell anyone about what he sees out there.'

McCoy straightened. 'Wait a minute! I don't mind a killin', that's what you hired me for, but Mann's a lawman, duly elected. I'll have every badge-toter along the border after my hide!'

Donovan held up one large hand. 'You won't. But Clayton will.'

It took only a moment for McCoy to realize what the big rancher was saying.

Then he smiled, nodding slowly. 'One way of makin' sure we get rid of him.'

'Damn right. Might even put a bounty on him. I mean, Lucas Mann's a good friend and, well, I gotta show some outrage, ain't I, if he gets himself killed?'

'Mal, you ain't lost your touch.'

CHAPTER 10

OUTRUN A BULLET

The Winchester was hot, but it wouldn't get much hotter; the box of cartridges Beef had given him was broken up beside him, spilling out less than half the number it had held – forty, he believed, but hadn't bothered to check the label, taking it as a standard-size box.

He beaded one of the Mexican boat crew, shot him through the right foot. He could hear the screams even way up here on the rock bluff above Turnabout Creek. The man danced frantically on the edge of the anchored riverboat, dropped the long plank he had been holding, then toppled into the murky water. He splashed frantically as the plank floated out of reach.

This caused more chaos and yelling and the rustlers shot at him from behind boulders and stunted brush. Clay returned fire with a three-shot volley, then ducked casually as lead whined off his shelter. He was too high and the angle was too steep for them to do him any harm.

But that could change and he fingered his six-gun belt loops, counting fourteen cartridges. With the Colt fully loaded, that meant twenty shots in all for the handgun. Maybe another twenty in the broken cardboard box beside him for the rifle.

The belt cartridges were .45 calibre but the rifle was .44.40; it would be another year or two before Colt developed a Peacemker model that would take the same calibre as the Winchester. So for now he had to make the best of what he had: twenty and twenty. Not bad odds. Not that good either! There were fewer than twenty men down there, including the mostly cowering crew of the paddlewheeler, but they were desperate and ruthless.

Well, maybe he could match them, both times.

It had seemed like a good idea at the time, to shoot up the riverboat men who were trying to slide the landing planks across to the bank where the cattle waited. If there was no means of getting the cows on board, then there was no cargo for the riverboat.

And no beef, meant hungry *rebeldes* or *bandidos*; two seemed pretty much interchangeable these days. Both wanted guns, but food was a priority over there in barren North Mexico. In fact, his last orders had stated clearly: *If you can't stop the guns, stop the food – starving men will soon decide they can't eat bullets.* So depriving them of either one would be worthwhile, both would be a victory.

113

He had been hoping the shooting would start a stampede but the cattle seemed mostly used to the sound of firearms and, while bawling and restless, did not break loose.

Which was too bad, for now he was alone, had been spotted, and was outnumbered by almost twenty to one.

The other thing was that once he stopped shooting from the high ground, which was his real advantage, they would come for him, no quarter asked or given.

So he decided not to waste what ammuntion he had left on the loading planks and the men who manipulated them; the boat would be a better target. He knew these old riverboats that worked the border rivers. Mostly they were owned by men who had no other interest than making the biggest profit for the smallest outlay; they were kept at the lowest possible operational level: bare wood being exposed to water rot and worm, wanting only a lick of paint or tar; rusty twin smokestacks, one each side, guyed up with wire, even patched with sheet tin held in place by more wire. The boiler room wouldn't bear inspection, if one he'd seen down in Durango was typical – and he figured it would have been. Steam hissing from fractured pipes and kinked tubing, worn washers on loose joints, boiler doors hanging by one hinge, the boilers themselves ancient relics salvaged from half-sunken wrecks in Campeche Bay.

So, the boat itself was a prime target; put it out of action and supplies and consignments of new guns were stopped dead, at least in this area, one of the biggest and most active smuggling points along the Rio Grande. It was his job to stop the guns any way he could.

He ducked as lead suddenly sent slivers of granite whizzing past his ear. Another bullet from below slammed into the rock edge bare inches from his face and he jerked back. But he had moved too fast; he lost his balance and yelled involuntarily as he spilled over the edge, frantically reaching for a hold with his left hand, his right clinging to his rifle.

It was a drop of almost twelve feet and there was one stunted bush growing out of a cleft about eight feet down. He let the rifle fall and snatched at the bush, feeling it tear at his palms and curling fingers. Teeth gritted, he emitted a snarling grunt as the jar came sooner than expected and his body whipped painfully. He lost his grip and dropped the rest of the way.

But the bush had broken his fall, although he still sprawled and bounced several times, landing on his right side – luckily! He lay there gasping. The rifle had landed between two floursack-sized rocks, the butt dented, a long splinter angled out from the cheek-piece. Otherwise it was ready to shoot as soon as he levered a shell into the breech.

But he was in trouble now. He had lost his main advantage, the high ground, and the carton of .44/.40 cartridges was either still up there or had fallen down the far side. Either way his firepower had been cut by at least half.

But he had one thing in his favour right now; if they

hadn't seen him fall – and it was quite possible they hadn't because of the steep angle the rustlers were viewing his rock from – then he could still get away. He had tethered the bay in the brush around the end of the big rock, only yards away.

Staggering, he was almost there when a familiar voice called, 'Just stay put, you son of a bitch! If that bay's been harmed, I'm takin' you in dead!'

The appearance of Lucas Mann stopped Clay in his tracks: he was the last man he expected to see. The sling supporting the man's left arm glared whitely, but the cocked Colt he held in his right hand was what drew Clay Emory's attention. He lifted his hands slightly out from his sides.

'I don't wear spurs. Your hoss ain't marked up, but I guess he's mighty tired. We did some hard ridin'.'

'That better be right. That you doing all the shooting?'

'Some. There's a bunch of rustlers and Mexes over the other side of the big rock. Mebbe they're on their way over here, looking for me by now.'

Mann seemed puzzled. 'How come you got mixed up in that kinda fracas? Figured you'd be well over the river by this time.'

'Me, too,' Clay told him wryly. 'But I saw the rustlers and followed them here. When I saw the riverboat, I figured I could stall 'em, or keep 'em from loading the cows on board at least.'

'And why the hell would you bother to do that?'

Clay was silent a few moments. 'That telegram you never sent. You were right. It was a code. "Counsellor

Worth" meant it would go straight to Fort Worth Ranger headquarters, no matter where you tried to send it to. The wording was just a brief outline of what I'd done so far on my mission.'

'Your . . . "mission"?'

'I'm not exactly a Ranger, Mann, but what they call the New Border Patrol is made up of equal numbers of Rangers and Mexican *delagados* – and the odd fast gun. Like me.'

'Which makes you an agent of what?'

'Mexican Government-sponsored border patrols, shared with the US. We're more interested in the guns that're being smuggled across than the rustled cattle, though the cows are important. If we stop them we stop the major part of the rebels' food.'

Mann stared, his gun still holding steady on Clay's mid-section. 'In other words, you're sayin' you're working under cover?'

'Yeah. We have dual jurisdiction, Mexico and the States. I've been working south of the Rio for months. My cover was blown and I had to go on the run. They drove me down into a part of Mexico I didn't know, which is how come I was desperate enough to hire someone like Miguel. My bad luck that he turned out to be part of the rebels' network bringing them guns,' He added, with a crooked smile, 'Though I think Miguel was more interested in Miguel than the rebel cause – once he realized I was carrying a large amount of *dinero,* anyway.'

'And which you got where?' Mann was struggling to absorb the information. But Clay was growing restless, expecting the rustlers to appear at any moment around the rock.

'Long story, Mann. Let's just say I found the money in a rebel stash and took it so they couldn't use it to pay for the next shipment of guns. But Donovan kept it anyway.'

Mann went very still. 'Big Mal's shipping guns to the Mex rebels?'

'Seems that way. I found a map which I used to trace the rebel cash. Someone had drawn in a rough sketch of Turnabout Creek with a dotted line straight to Broken D.'

Breath hissed through Mann's teeth. 'You can prove all this?'

'If you'd sent that telegraph message I could.'

Mann grunted, then suddenly jerked his gun. 'Let me see my horse while I think about it.'

'We better think about gettin' outta here. Those rustlers'll be this side of the creek by now, looking for a way around this rock. Did you come alone?'

'I aimed to. But I stopped at Broken D to get a decent mount and – well, I'm pretty sure Mal sent McCoy after me. But I think I may've lost him.'

'Goddammit, Mann, you were stupid not to bring a posse!'

They were almost at the corner around which Clay had left the bay tethered by now. Just as they reached it Reece McCoy and three armed men appeared, the gunfighter smiling crookedly at the startled look on Clay's and Mann's faces.

'So, you're a lousy Gov'ment agent, Emory!' McCoy

said, his voice full of confidence. 'Mal will be pleased to know *that*!' When Clay said nothing, McCoy cupped his left hand behind his ear, the Colt in his other hand steadying threateningly. The men with him also held their guns ready.

'What? Nothin' to say? Aw, hell! What about you, Mann?'

'I'm still trying to work things out,' the sheriff said succinctly. His gun was down at his side and the hammer was still cocked under his thumb. 'If those rustlers are Broken D rannies, you're the one had better do the talkin', McCoy.'

Reece McCoy smiled without humour. 'Well, seein' as you're startin' to get a handle on things, I'd better put a stop to that.'

Suddenly his gun roared in two fast shots and Lucas Mann reeled back, staggering for three or four paces before his legs folded and he crumpled to the ground.

Clay brought up his Colt but paused when he found himself looking down the smoking barrel of McCoy's gun, which was backed by the other three men with their weapons at the ready.

Another man came panting up, his clothes torn, a few leaves and twigs still clinging to them from where he had forced his way through the brush. He was tall and rangy, bearded, his hair a light brown, almost ginger.

'Judas priest, Mac! What the hell've you done!' he pointed his six-gun at the dead sheriff. 'Big Mal'll have your balls, killin' a lawman! You know he's always been agin that because of the stink it makes.'

McCoy turned eyes still bright with the thrill of killing in the rangy man's direction. 'You worry about gettin' them cows on to the riverboat, Ringo. Leave this to me.'

'Gladly! Sure as hell wouldn't want to be in your boots when you try to explain to Mal what you done.'

McCoy surprised them by smiling. Then he swung his gaze to Clay and pointed with his still smoking gun barrel.

'Hell, I din' kill Mann. Was Clay Emory done it. Ask anyone here. We was just too late to stop it, weren't we, boys?'

The three Broken D men who had come with McCoy nodded, one man saying,

'Was Emory done it, all right.'

Ringo frowned. 'I heard enough to know you better not kill *him*! Jesus, Mac! A Gov'ment agent! You'd never get away with it. The place'll be crawlin' with marshals and rangers, and how's Donovan gonna get his guns across the Rio with all that law stompin' on his toes?'

'Shut up, you damn fool!' McCoy snarled and for a moment Ringo's face was grey where the beard didn't cover the flesh. Obviously he thought McCoy was going to shoot him.

The gunfighter heaved a sigh and lowered the hammer on his gun. Ringo relaxed noticeably.

'You're right, of course. Kill Clay and we've got more trouble than a bed full of rattlers. But how're we s'posed to know he's a Gov'ment man? Huh?' He looked around him, eyebrows arched. 'Anyone hear him say he works for the rangers or this new border patrol? All we know is, he escaped jail in town an' right here in front of us, when poor ol' Lucas catches up with him, why, he guns him down in cold blood. Then makes a run for it! On a hoss he'd already stole from Lucas. Lit out like a Fourth of July rocket.' He shook his head slowly. 'Damn Saddlebacks! Helluva place for a manhunt. But when we do catch up with him and shoot him down, he's just a murderin' snake far as we're concerned.' He cupped a hand to his left ear again, and his voice rose to a falsetto. 'What's that, Marshal? An undercover agent for the border patrol! Oh, Lordy, Lordy, what've we done! No one told us. *Sorrrieeee*!'

All the guns swung to cover Clay as he waited, tensed. McCoy continued to grin.

'Leather that there Colt, Clay. Go on! Now, climb aboard the bay and start ridin'. We'll give you a leetle start, then we'll be right behind you. You'll be dead by noon. That's a promise. Now *git*!'

The gunfighter put another slug into the ground near Clay's boots and Clay swung swiftly aboard the patient bay, kicking his heels into the flanks and racing away around the giant rock, the bay skidding a little.

Ringo yelled, 'How big a start we gonna give him?'

'Aw . . . reckon that's far enough!'

McCoy brought his gun up blazing; the others were caught napping, not having their own guns ready to shoot soon enough.

Clay heard the *whipppp!* of McCoy's bullet and he

121

rolled in the saddle, sliding down to the far side, reins wrapped about his hand, feet straining in one stirrup iron, right boot atop the other. His Colt blasted, just two quick shots. The group down there scattered, one man dropping to his knees, hands pressed against his midriff.

Taken by surprise at Clay's accuracy, the Broken D men dived for cover. McCoy, having slid behind a deadfall, rose up now, his gun seeking the fugitive. He looked around wildly.

'Goddammit! Where the hell'd he disappear to?' he raged, seeing only a cloud of dust where Clay had been a moment ago.

'Judas, Mac!' said Ringo. 'I hope we can catch up with him! You realize what it'd be like havin' to tell Mal you gave him a start and it was big enough for him to give us the slip?'

McCoy scowled. 'Shut up! An' get after him.'

But sweat drenched his suddenly pale face.

What Ringo had just said didn't bear thinking about.

CHAPTER 11

MANHUNT

Beef called in two of the men who had been branding
Rectangle 5 cattle for most of the afternoon, Dreamy
and Potch. They were trail-pards, early thirties,
drifters, working the ranch circuit at round-up time,
careful to make sure they had a job to see them
through each winter.

And they were damn good workers, men who knew
their way about cattle country and did their best to
keep their employers happy. They were both ex-army,
Dreamy claiming to have been the best tracker in his
outfit. Beef had no cause to doubt him; the man had
tracked down stray cattle and horses several times,
finding sign where others had searched and given up.
And that included a full-blood Comanche scout.

Potch was the tough guy: a man who could hold his
liquor, but he liked it too well at times, enjoyed a fight
or two almost as much as he did a couple of bottles of
redeye.

'You boys're about done here an' Mattie's happy enough with your work. She told me to find you some jobs if you fancied stayin' on. . . ?' He let it drift off into a question. 'Somethin' you could stretch into winter, mebbe.' He paused and they glanced at each other. Dreamy answered.

'We like the cook,' he said and that was as good a reply as Beef expected to hear; if a man liked the grub he was served up he'd do a good day's work. 'OK, Potch?'

'He keeps them flapjacks an' treacle comin', I'll stay.'

Beef nodded, face deadpan as usual. '*Bueno*. Meantime, there's a special chore Mattie wants done.'

'Only gotta ask.'

Beef studied their rugged faces, the hard-muscled bodies, honed from honest labour, men as tough as the brush-bred cattle they worked with. 'You know our head count's down – way down, this season. We got our suspicions why—'

'Hell, a blind man could tell you why!' Potch interrupted, sniffing loudly through a big nose that divided his narrow face like a hatchet blade. 'We ain't been pickin' up near as many mavericks as we should.'

Dreamy answered in that lazy drawl he affected, 'Wonder why, when Broken D's maverick tally is way up?'

Beef nodded. 'Too bad Donovan's too big for us to ride over and insist we check his herds. But, fact is – an' you better keep this to yourselves – Mattie's way behind with the mortgage. Now Donovan's got

124

himself elected to the board of the goddam bank, and word is they're hintin' about foreclosin' . . . at Big Mal's suggestion, of course.'

'Hell you say! Land-grabbin' son of a bitch!'

'Big Mal's gettin' ready to move in, right?' said Potch, grim-faced. 'Showin' his hand at last.'

'We seen it comin', but wasn't expectin' it so soon. Mattie, bein' the good-hearted soul she is, figured he'd be gennleman enough to give her some breathin' space.'

Potch spat. 'Heard he's got his sights on the Governor's mansion in Austin. Guess the more of Texas he owns, the better he figures his chances of election.'

'Yeah,' Beef agreed. 'An' if you b'lieve Clayton, Mal's got his hands on a good deal of money.'

'Where we goin' with this, Beef?' Dreamy asked suddenly, his droopy eyelids half-closed as they usually were when he was thinking hard, whether it be about the best way of chousing a maverick out of the chaparral or where to hit an opponent to end a fight and get back to the serious business of drinking.

It surprised him to see Beef suddenly uncertain – this, in a man who never held any doubts about his actions, a range boss with a top reputation for quick, decisive thinking.

'Dunno whether Mattie's taken a shine to this Clay, or if it's just that she's got a dig from her conscience, figuring she mighta done him wrong all those years ago when he got her folks killed.'

'She blamed him for that?'

125

'Yeah. She was young, near hysterical, an' figured – well, hell, I dunno what she figured! But she's got it into her head that Donovan's out to kill him. Accordin' to Clay, Big Mal stole a heap of *dinero* from him and a couple of townsfolk swear it was McCoy duckin' away from the jailhouse after the shootin' when Clay busted out. We know a Broken D bunch is huntin' for him, with McCoy leadin' the pack. Seein' as you two are such good trackers, Mattie'd like you to try to get to Clay first, and bring him back to Rectangle. There'll be a few extra bucks in it, for you, of course.'

'Thought she was broke?' Potch allowed.

'Not broke, more damaged I guess. But you know her: she won't be obligated to anyone. She wants a job like this done, she'll find some way of payin' up. An' squarely. Now that's about all I know. You want the chore or not?'

He looked directly at Potch who said, 'Lemme think about it. Over a pile of Cooky's flapjacks an' treacle.'

'You just want an excuse to fill your belly,' Dreamy said with maybe a hint of a smile twitching his wide mouth. 'As for me, I ain't got no trouble makin' up my mind. But I might take time to give it some deep thought – just to be sure, you know? Reckon Cooky could find me a slice of his deep-dish apple pie I can munch on while I'm makin' real sure, Beef?'

It was hell's own luck that he was loose in strange country once again.

Seemed like he had been travelling for months through a land he didn't know, going by instinct, following nature's signs, hoping he didn't run into a bunch of rebels who would slit his throat for his worn riding-boots and likely shoot his eyes out just for the hell of it. And another bunch, even more bloodthirsty, somewhere behind him.

For about the hundredth time he wondered whether he had suffered some kind of brain storm when he had finally accepted the chief ranger's deal all those years ago.

'Perfect set up, Clay,' the big, moustachioed man with the shoulder-length dark hair had said, one hand lightly stroking his goatee beard. 'Hard luck on the old folks killed in that buckboard pile-up, but suits us to hear how 'most everyone figures you for being a trigger-happy lawman who ought've known better than to carry a gunfight on to Main Street where citizens were.'

Clay was surly, annoyed things were turning out this way; he liked Fremont, and the sheriff's job; but he knew he was finished there now, as sheriff or anything else, after that gunfight with the Bellmans.

The chief stared back calmly. 'Thing is, we've been watching you for some time; our man recommended we ask you to join the New Border Patrol. Ah, you can look surprised but you've got what we're looking for. We need a man across the Rio in a hurry, someone with a bounty on his head – not too big, or some Mex'll try to collect and that's not the idea at all.'

Clay was more than half-interested now. 'Well, what is the idea?'

'You're about to be stuck for five grand compensation, due to the next of kin of those old folk who were killed. Oh, we can stop it any time, but it happens it's just what we need now. You make a run across the Rio. We put out a fugitive warrant for you absconding from a legal debt and . . . what've we got?'

'Me! On the run in *mañana* land! With empty pockets and a crick in my neck from lookin' over my shoulder for some bravo tryin' to put a bullet in my back!'

The chief ranger smiled slowly. 'Exactly! A man with law snapping at his heels, a man good with a gun, short of *dinero*. Just the kind of fella who might be inclined to join up with rebels or *bandidos* or – gringos running guns.'

'Not my kinda deal, Marshal.'

'Wrong. You went under cover when you were in the army and broke up that white slave ring. This is the same kind of thing. Oh, maybe a mite more dangerous, but. . . .'

And he'd been loco enough to agree. Mind, the pay for tackling such a dangerous mission was more than five times what he could earn as a town lawman, anywhere.

The chances of getting killed, of course, were more likely ten times as much, which was why the pay was so good. At least it'd be something different – and worthwhile, but not anything he'd want as a career. Still. . . .

He'd gone in with his eyes wide open and somehow had survived for over five years, south of the border, mixing with all kinds of murderous men – and a few women who could outdo them with knife or gun.

He had been directly responsible for smashing at least three major gun-running rings, and had managed to sabotage several shipments of illegal weapons.

He was lucky to still have his head on his shoulders. But now he was in more danger than he could shake a stick at – in his home state, and in country he barely knew.

There would be no chance this time to fast-talk his way past suspicious, mean-eyed cut-throats. This time he would be shot on sight, on Big Mal Donovan's orders.

As the thought formed he hipped in the saddle while the bay drank at a scummy pool. He stiffened when he saw riders on the slope behind working their mounts down towards him. They were coming fast: there was no doubt they had spotted him and weren't wasting any time.

Curse the luck! Or lack of it!

He had less than a two-mile lead.

Already the bay was feeling the strain of trying to make good time through these skewed and crumbling hills. It was a damn fine horse, the way it picked its way through all the obstacles, moving around sharp rocks, pausing to make sure there were no sleeping snakes on the far side of a deadfall before stepping over, staying a few feet out from low-hanging branches or heavy brush. Lucas Mann had trained it well.

Except it was a mite too cautious, with those sonu-vers closing in on him.

So he had no choice; he dug in his bootheels and the bay snorted and lurched forward, rolling an accusing eye at its rider even as weary muscles knotted, ready for yet another speedy run.

No wonder Mann had come after the animal: it was all heart and deserved to survive this deadly tiggy-touch-wood kind of pursuit.

Clay just hoped the horse would be fast enough to outrun the bullets about to come his way.

CHAPTER 12

BETTER'N BULLETS

Because of the timber and the random brush growth, he wasn't sure how many men were coming: only that there weren't as many as McCoy had had with him.

So that meant they had split up. OK, say he was seeing about half of McCoy's bunch. Where the hell was the other half?

McCoy would know this country. The Saddlebacks were practically a part of Broken D, and had at one time been owned by Donovan. But way back, when Big Mal was truly short of cash and needed to show the colour of his *dinero* to buy seed bulls, he had sold the Saddlebacks to Mattie's father.

At the time Donovan didn't care why Old Man Carr wanted that collection of dreary, mankilling giant rocks and twisted vegetation. The cash was his main

131

concern and he bought his bulls and upgraded the quality of his herds, determined that Broken D would have the best beef in Texas.

His ego was large enough to match his massive build at that time, and had only blunted slightly over the ensuing years. But he had been mighty startled when he realized that Jonas Carr had blasted through a couple of arroyos and suddenly there were two arms of Turnabout Creek: one with the Rio running into it, and now the other, a good sixty feet lower in elevation, with the creek's outflow meeting the river on the far side of those timber-clad rocks. The Saddlebacks were big enough to be called mountains by the locals, and death traps for any cattle that strayed into them.

But Carr hadn't wanted more land for his cows; he merely wanted the water. He diverted it to feed his own section of barren plain where Rectangle 5 bled off into the Saddlebacks: flat, dead-dry dust and gravel. *Until.* . . .

Donovan, working to his own arrogant agenda of building the biggest and best cattle ranch in Texas, hadn't even taken any notice when the blasting started. Only some months later, when McCoy reported that Rectangle 5's plains were now deep and green with lush feed and Carr was driving his herds in, did the truth dawn on Big Mal. Carr had used the extra arm of Turnabout Creek to irrigate the dead land! Goddammit! Who would've thought old man Carr had enough brains to do that!

It made Big Mal grind his teeth as he watched Carr's cows slap on condition at a rate he didn't believe possible. And when the Five, as locals called it, outdid him in the price meat agents were paying for beef on the hoof, Donovan drank himself senseless on a couple of bottles of the Demon.

He had tried to buy back the Saddlebacks, moving in fast after Mattie's parents were killed, but she wouldn't sell. But now . . . he could smile wryly as he studied his wall map and tapped the Saddleback area with a gnarled finger.

'See if you change your mind when the bank starts foreclosure, you bitch,' he murmured, confident that Mattie would have no choice but to sell to him, and for *his* price.

Clay knew nothing about Donovan's plans for the Saddlebacks, but he did know their brief history and that he was about to be trapped here while he was low on ammunition. There wasn't a hope in hell that he could expect anything but a miserable death from McCoy and his hardcases.

So, if he didn't have bullets to spare he would just have to find some other way of stopping them.

As he paused to think about his problem, he realized how painful his left side was. He was concerned to find that his shirt on that side and the waistband of his trousers were soaked with his blood. When he twisted in the saddle again, he winced and became aware of the sharp, tearing feeling in the long knife wound. Obviously it was splitting open with all his exertions.

Not only that, there were bright drops of blood spattering the ground here and there.

'Like a goddamn signpost!' he gritted, swinging the

bay into some trees, lifting it just in time to clear a deadfall. He swore softly when he saw that the slope he had chosen was littered with deadfalls, some lying across the ground, the trees that had wrenched free of the soil leaning against others still standing. Maybe caused by the blasting years ago; no one would have bothered clearing the slope, for only the course of the creek below had been important at the time.

But some of these downed trees were jammed cross-wise with others still growing, and a couple looked mighty precarious, held, apparently, only by some steeply canted slim saplings, acting like supporting stakes.

He took a quick line of sight back down the blood trail he had only just become aware of leaving. *If he could loosen a couple of those saplings. . . .*

It was right above the trail along which he could expect the men hunting him to come; they wouldn't be blind to the bright-red spots and smears, so he could predict where they would appear.

There was a lariat on the bay's saddle horn and even while he was thinking out his plan he started uncoiling it. He tossed it with an old skill acquired many years ago when he was just a working stiff on a border ranch, and dropped the loop over the nearest stake. A quick dally round the horn, a touch of his boot heels and a quiet but firm, '*Back up, boy!*' and the earth moved around the base of the sapling.

Then it erupted and the deadfall's weight slid down a couple of feet, forcing the sapling almost horizontal.

He released the pressure in time to keep it at a

134

rising angle, even though it was trembling under the weight of the big log. He paused and, through the blood pounding in his ears, he heard horses making their way up the trail.

One more stake loosened and that would do it.

'Hey, there's the sonuver now!'

The shouted words startled him and he saw riders heaving up another trail that he hadn't noticed, joining up with McCoy and his group on their trail.

Guns blazed and lead whipped air around him, two slugs tearing bark from the second, dangerously leaning deadfall. More guns opened up and he felt the bay stagger; he figured this had to be it: *right now!* No more time for planning.

The lurch as lead seared the bay's rump was enough to yank the supporting sapling from under the dead-fall. Dirt erupted, timber creaked and splintered and the bay snorted, dancing as it fought to keep its footing. Bullets were still whistling around Clay as he yanked the horse's head around and urged it across the steeply angled slope – right out from under the erupting deadfalls, three of which burst loose simultaneously.

This started a small avalanche, the rumbling, crashing sounds of which drowned the wild, panicky yells of McCoy and his men as they saw what must have looked like the whole damn mountain coming down on top of them.

Clay struggled to keep the horse more or less upright while it still fought for a more secure footing. He was in time to see a couple of tons of earth and rocks and massive logs ploughing and juggernauting down the slope, tearing loose half the mountainside, thick clouds of roiling dust trailing in the wake.

The bay was whickering, prancing, frightened, and Clay kept talking to it, patting its neck, keeping tension on the reins as he watched the landslide he had created wipe out McCoy's hardcases: horses and men all atangle, half-buried in the deadly slide as it piled up at last on a more level section.

'Better'n bullets,' Clay commented half-aloud, standing now beside the quivering horse, getting it calmed down. He saw the fresh bullet burn across its right hip; it would slow the animal, likely hurt some for a while, but it wouldn't kill or cripple him.

Leading the bay, he slowly picked his way around the carnage below and was almost clear when he saw movement among the tangled bodies.

Reece McCoy reared up, left arm obviously broken, hanging loose and bloody down at his side, more blood smearing his face, shirt half-torn from his body. He didn't say anything, just lifted his Colt with surprising speed considering his condition and fired. The bullet came close enough to tear Clay's hat from his head, then he was down on one knee, triggering his own Colt even as McCoy got off his second shot.

The lead drove into the bank beside Clay and he instinctively flung himself away, rolling on to his side and shooting across his body – his last bullet in the Colt. McCoy was already slumping, chin almost down on his chest where fresh blood spurted. But he still lifted his smoking gun and took one more shot at Clay.

He missed by a mile because the barrel was pointing skyward; then the gunfighter sprawled and bounced once before sliding down several feet on his face, crashing into a rock.

Clay stood there, half-slumped against the nervous bay, his smoking gun dangling.

'By Godfrey, we don't need trackers to find you!' a voice said slightly above where he stood, startling him. 'Just look for the nearest corner of Hell – and there you are!'

Clay managed to turn and just before he fell, said, 'Well, howdy, Beef. Glad to – seeeee ya. . . .'

Beef and Potch hurried forward and Dreamy said, 'We still gonna get paid for findin' him, Beef? I mean, we only had to track him up the other slope and then he – kinda led us right to him with all this ruckus.'

'How about a second helpin' of flapjacks 'n' treacle?' Beef suggested.

He was surprised when both Dreamy and Potch grinned and nodded. 'Sounds fair,' they chorused.

'Done. Now we better pick him up before he slides away like McCoy. He don't look all that chipper, do he?'

Six men had died in that deadly slide: count McCoy, actually dying from Clay's bullet, and the tally was seven.

Even Big Mal Donovan would feel such a loss, though he still had plenty of men riding for Broken D. But Beef had told Clay earlier that most of these were just straight cowhands, earning an honest living working the huge ranch.

'Which don't mean he can't come up with a handful of hardcases if he needs to,' Beef cautioned.

Dreamy and Potch had been pulling bodies out of the pile of dirt and splintered logs; now Dreamy wiped a soiled neckerchief around his dirt-smeared face and said,

'Hey, Beef, Ringo ain't among them bodies. I swear I seen him ridin' with McCoy's bunch when we topped out on that ridge earlier.'

'Yeah, he was with 'em all right,' confirmed Potch, hands on hips, looking around at the chaotic confusion of the slope. He pointed suddenly. 'There's a rock ledge juttin' out under all that dirt an' rubble. I seen Ringo on a grey hoss there. He could be under it, knocked out or somethin'.'

Clay, being the nearest to the cluttered ledge, started down a little gingerly. Beef had wrapped a clean undershirt from his own saddle-bags around his torso and buttoned what was left of Clay's shirt over it to hold it firmly in place.

He felt a little more blood oozing from the long, shallow cut as he steadied himself against a canted tree, and eased forward on to the dirt and rubble piled up on the ledge.

He crawled forward, the dirt loose and tending to allow his hands and forearms to sink into it. But he got to the edge and looked over. He turned his head and called to the others.

'He's down there. Dunno if he's alive or not. There's a tree across one of his legs. Looks crushed to me and he's not moving so I guess he's—'

'I – I'm alive – you sonuverbitch!' the big brown-haired man croaked, spitting dirt as it rolled from his bloody face into his mouth. 'Git this – tree offa – me!'

Clay nodded gently. From what he could see the tree was huge, immovable, and the only way Ringo could hope to get free was if his leg was removed.

By now Beef had worked his way down. Clay pointed out the mangled leg even as Ringo cussed the both of them. Beef pursed his lips, then took a heavy-bladed hunting knife from his belt sheath and began to strop it across the loose end of his gunbelt.

Ringo saw this and stopped cursing, mouth agape, as he looked slowly from the knife to his crushed leg.

'*Noooooo!*' he roared, the word echoing around the mountainside. 'Get the hell away from me with that!'

'Up to you, Ringo,' Beef said slowly, still stropping the blade. 'Might be the four of us could lift the tree off you but your leg's restin' on solid rock so we can't dig you out. We do nothin', an' you'll die soon's the sun goes down and the wolves get a scent of all the blood. Your decision. I've done amputations before. I won't make too big a mess of it, 'long as we can stop the bleedin'.'

'He's passed out,' Clay Emory said quietly.

'Well,' Beef said grimly, feeling the now well-honed edge of the knife. 'Might as well make a start.'

'Wait,' said Potch. 'I reckon we *could* lift that tree enough so's we could pull him out. See that flat rock beside it? We get one of them saplings lyin' around and lever it up; only needs to be for an inch or two.'

139

'He'll still lose the leg,' Beef pointed out when the others agreed with Potch. 'But we could mebbe get him in to the sawbones. Not sure he'd make it, though.'

'Wait!' They all frowned at Clay's curtness. 'We can ease the tree up enough to drag him out, I reckon. Be a helluva job but we can likely do it. But Ringo don't need to know that – yet.'

All three men stared. 'The hell you sayin'?' demanded Beef.

Clay looked back soberly. 'Ringo was next down the line to McCoy. He'll know when Donovan's expecting the next load of guns. I need to know that.'

Beef said flatly, 'Ringo ain't all that bad. Not like McCoy.'

'It's my job, Beef. I need that information. If he's smart he'll tell me in a few minutes, then we can—'

'It's true what they say, ain't it?' Beef cut in. 'Once a badge-toter, never a man! You sonuverbitch!'

140

CHAPTER 13

GUNS

'You think I'm bein' hard on Ringo?'

The answer was plain enough in the way Beef and the others looked at Clay.

'He may not be as bad as McCoy but he's part of Donovan's gun runners and rustlers. He's an outlaw and I'd say he's done his share of killing.' He held up as hand as Potch made to speak. 'When I finally got them white slavers on the run they went up the Rio del Poco, a very narrow river, in a side-wheeler. We chased 'em in a stern-wheeler and started to overtake. But we had to stop half a dozen times because the bodies of the young girls the bastards threw overside kept getting caught up in our paddlewheel.'

'Judas!' breathed Dreamy and Potch grimaced as he imagined the scene. Beef said, 'Ringo ain't a white slaver.'

'No. But those are the kind of people Donovan's

dealing with. They don't care about the rebels so-called cause. They buy the guns from Donovan and sell 'em to anyone who can pay, after they remove the firing pins. Then they sell *those*. Buyers've got no comeback. Guns are no good without firing pins.'

'Well, I dunno nothin' about the Mexican troubles,' admitted Dreamy, 'an' don't wanta, but I wouldn't do business with the kinda snakes you're talkin' about.'

After a moment or two Potch nodded and Beef scrubbed a hand around his jaw. 'So you aim to stop the guns at any cost?'

'That's my job, Beef, and no one's gonna stop me doing it, sure not just because one of the gunrunnin' gang has to suffer for a few more minutes.'

Beef pursed his lips as he looked into Clay's steely stare. 'You're a hard bastard, Clayton.'

Clay smiled crookedly and knelt beside Ringo, who was coming out of his daze. 'Ringo, if we bust a gut, we *might* be able to lift the log enough so's we can slide you out from under.'

Hope flashed on the trapped man's congested face.'Then – blame well – do it!'

Clay scratched the side of his nose slowly. 'We need you to help us out a little first, though.'

Ringo rolled puzzled eyes to the others, then back to Clay. 'The hell you on about? Just get me outta here!'

'All you gotta do is tell me about the next shipment of guns.'

Ringo suddenly looked very wary. 'What guns?'

'The ones Donovan's running across the Rio. Come

on, Ringo! Your chances of keeping that leg are runnin' out by the minute.'

'Christ! I – I dunno nothin' about any guns!'

'You damn fool! Donovan won't care about you hoppin' about on one leg. You'll get no rewards for loyalty. And if you don't hurry things up you could die, that right, Beef?'

Beef didn't like being drawn into it this way. He glared, then lifted his knife. 'We shouldn't wait any longer, Ringo. Might already be too late.'

The trapped man's chest was heaving now, his eyes wild as he looked at the four deadpan faces staring at him. When sunlight flashed from Beef's knife he suddenly said, half-shouting, 'All *right*! All right. I'll tell you what I know. Just – get me outta here!'

'You've got our words, Ringo,' Clay said.

Ringo swivelled his gaze from one to the other, asked for and got a drink of water, and then began to talk. Clay bent close so that he didn't miss a word.

'I could kind of . . . pull rank and *order* you to put your men under my authority, Mattie.'

Mattie Carr's lovely face was set in grim lines as her head snapped up, her eyes glistening with warning signs.

'*Order* me! Just who do you think you are, Clay?'

'I'm a member of the New Border Patrol with the same standing as a federal marshal, Mattie. It's not anything I want to force upon people, but the authority is there if I need to use it.'

Her eyes narrowed more if anything. 'You ride back

from the Saddlebacks, after destroying half a mountain if I'm to believe Beef, killing or maiming at least
ten men, and now you bring back one of Donovan's
men so badly injured he'll very likely lose his leg – or
his life! *Then* you tell me you can *order* me to send my
men with you!'

Clay nodded slowly. 'That's what I'm saying,
Mattie.'

They were on the front porch of Rectangle 5,
Mattie's hands still blood-smeared from having given
the unconscious Ringo what help she could. He was
being made as comfortable as possible in a buckboard
now, ready to be driven into town to the doctor, in the
hope that his mangled leg could be saved. If not –
well, at least he would probably live.

'I can't order my men to go with you! I *won't* if you
prefer. They're cowhands, Clay, not soldiers!'

'You told me once that nearly every man working
for the Five had seen service in the Army during the
war.'

'But it's peacetime now!'

'Here, it's peacetime. Just across the river there's a
war going on. You might not think it's any affair or
ours and I don't pretend to know the rights or wrongs
of it, Mattie, or the ethics, but we can't be accused of
supplying guns to the rebels, freely or otherwise. It
comes down to politics, Mattie; these things always do.
I have to stop the guns reaching the rebels, or the
bandits who pose as genuine rebels. I need your help,
and I'm asking for it – first as a friend, but if you refuse
then I'll have to. . . .'

'Pull rank. Yes, you made that very clear.' She seemed calmer now, though, and studied his face carefully. 'You're a strange man, Clay Emory. I know you stand by your word. And I haven't found you to be a . . . liar. But you'll have to leave it up to the men. I won't order them to risk their lives by helping you. But if they want to help, then it's up to them.' She softened her tone a little. 'That's the best I can do, Clay. Don't ask more of me.'

'I'm obliged, Mattie.'

He started to turn away and she placed a hand on his arm. 'I'm sorry, Clay. It's the way I feel. I can't *order* my men to risk their lives. I couldn't have it on my conscience.'

He smiled faintly. 'I understand, Mattie. I agree that it's only fair they make up their own minds.'

He felt her fingers tighten briefly on his arm. 'Six years ago . . . I had you all wrong didn't I?'

'We were both different then,' he said off-handedly. He touched a hand to the brim of his bullet-punctured hat and started towards the bunkhouse where the crew of Rectangle 5 were ready to have supper.

They watched him carefully as he sat down at a table away from the main one and the cook set a plate of stew and biscuits before him. He felt their eyes on his every movement.

He didn't keep them in suspense. He wolfed down the meal – the best he had tasted in a coon's age – wiped his mouth and rolled a cigarette. Through the first exhalation of smoke he asked,

'How many of you want to come with me and help

145

me stop Big Mal Donovan running guns into Mexico?'

No answers at first, then a redhead at the far end of the table said, 'Ain't our problem, feller.'

There were murmurs that concurred with the redhead's reply.

'Mebbe not,' Clay admitted. 'Unless the rebs get the upper hand; then north Mexico, just across that river you can see from right outside that door, is in the hands of rabble, drunk on victory and as much tequila as they can lay hands to. You figure the width of the Rio is enough to keep 'em from coming across and seein' what the good ol' *Americanos* have got over here that they might have better use for? You can count on it includin' women as well as cattle, *dinero* and anything else in between. Anyone tries to stop 'em better make out his will first. There'll be no law to keep 'em on their side of the river and by the time those same good ol' *americano* politicos push all kinds of legal bills through Congress, and just maybe get the go-ahead to cross the Rio and kick the asses of those rebs, well, quite a lot of damage could be done. You fellers think about it.'

'*You* think about it,' called the redhead. 'We're just poor dumb bastards of cowhands tryin' to earn a livin', such as it is. We're too blamed tired at the end of the day to worry about greasers killin' each other. Anyway, the more the merrier, I reckon.'

There was a chorus of agreement and when the catcalling and smart remarks died down, one man asked, 'How you know Big Mal's smugglin' guns anyway?'

'Ringo told me. And I've been working under cover

for years. Not long back I got a line that a pick-up place for guns was at Manzano Point, on Broken D, which has a damn long river frontage as you know. You've heard how Miguel Delesandro tried to poison me; then Slim Norton, one of your own top hands on the take, bought into it, and finally, two of Donovan's men, Shorty and Tower tried to make sure I couldn't throw a spanner in the works. If I'd had any doubts about him before, I sure didn't after that.'

'Before or after you killed the lot of 'em?' someone shouted.

'It was them or me. There's another angle, too. Donovan's been stealing the Five's mavericks and rustling your branded cattle. He sells 'em to the rebels to keep 'em fed. He not only makes a profit there, but he reduces the Five's stock, leaves Mattie with not enough cows to sell and pay her mortgage. You can figure what happens next. You won't be trying to make a living on Rectangle 5 then; you'll be workin' for Big Mal or not at all.'

That brought on an animated discussion and much swearing and genuine anger. Then someone cleared his throat and said loudly, 'Sounds to me like you're kinda more serious about this than we allowed, Clayton.'

'Nothing like a dose of rat poison with your *frijoles*, or a knife in the ribs to make you lose your sense of humour,' Clay allowed. 'Yeah, I'm damn serious about this.'

There was low-voiced, earnest discussion after that. Once again Clay was surprised at its brevity.

147

'How many men you need?' was the first question.

'We get extra pay for helpin' you out?'

'Just how blamed dangerous is it, anyway?'

He knew he had them then: their interest was aroused, even if they did try to disguise it with levity.

In the end, eight men volunteered to back him, including Beef, Dreamy and Potch. A few others were undecided.

Mattie agreed to take a telegraph message into town when she accompanied Ringo to the doctor's and have it sent to Counsellor Worth, advising of the situation. Clay explained it was a code address for his chief.

'Mebbe it'll all be over by the time he can get men in here, but he has to know, whichever way it turns out. I can't wait for official approval before making a move. Those guns are due in tonight, according to Ringo.'

His words brought a frown to her face and he thought maybe she paled slightly. 'You really need more men, I think, Clay.'

'Always,' he said with a fleeting smile. 'But you get that message off to the chief while I put these men in the picture.'

She hesitated, then said quietly, 'Take care, Clay Emory.'

'That's how I've made it this far.' He grinned.

She watched him walk away, bullet scar on the face, limping, rubbing his wounded side, his clothes looking as if he had been dragged through chaparral

148

at the end of a rope behind a galloping horse.

Yes – this far, she told herself, and her teeth tugged at her full bottom lip. How much more could any man take and still be eager to do his job?

Counting himself, Clay reckoned there should be nine men in total. But there were ten.

Puzzled, he counted again in the dark down beyond the corrals, then saw the redheaded cowboy who had been so vocal in the bunkhouse standing hipshot, thumbs hooked into his gunbelt. 'Joining us after all?' he asked.

'Figured I better put my gun where my mouth is,' the redhead offered by way of explanation. 'They call me "Red".'

'I'd never have guessed.' Clay grinned as they shook hands briefly. 'Thanks, Red.'

'Where we headed?'

'The river – where else?'

Red looked up at the stars and the first glow of a rising moon. 'Nice night for a swim.'

'Not if you've got any lead weighing you down.'

'Hell! You tryin' to get me to change my mind?'

'Just trying to impress on all of you that this is not going to be any picnic. I'd be happier with twice as many men. We'll be going up agin Donovan's crew, as well as the Mex *contrabandistas.*'

'Hell! Why din' you say so!'

Red hurried off. When he returned fifteen minutes later he had six more men with him.

'How did you get—?' Clay began, but Red cut in,

149

'Used my powers of persuasion.'

It was about then that Clay noticed two men with bloody kerchiefs held to their noses, another rubbing his jaw and still another. . . . But by then he savvied Red's 'powers of peruasion'.

'I kind a mentioned a bonus, too.'

'You might have to pay that out of your own pocket if my chief don't agree. But let's get going,' Clay said, feeling more confident now as they, mounted up.

CHAPTER 14

BATTLE AT MANZANO

The night shook with the thunder of an explosion. Above the blurred outline of a hill some way ahead they saw the sky light up as if with a lightning strike.

They hauled rein, hands automatically straying to their guns. Clay, slightly ahead, calmed the big bay which seemed to sense danger because of that rumble, distinct from the rolling thunder of a storm. He held up one hand as the men behind him fought skittish mounts.

'The hell was that?' someone asked hoarsely.

The query was echoed a dozen times before Clay told them about the run-in with the *bandidos'* riverboat attempting to pick up rustled cattle from Broken D's rannies. 'Their boat ran aground on the Manzano Bank. I figure it must've blocked the entrance to the

151

creek where they're waiting to load the guns. The boat's due about now. That sounded like dynamite, so I reckon they're blasting the wreck to clear the entrance.'

'Might be a good time to hit 'em – while they're busy, huh?' Beef suggested but Clay was already urging the bay forward, waving his arm for the others to follow.

Like a dark tide the bunch of armed men swept up the slope, their mounts making a muted thunder of their own.

They did not pause as they topped the crest, glimpsing moonlight reflecting from convulsing water that spattered into a hundred small eruptions as shattered timbers fell out of the sky. Flames flickered, subsided, broke out anew in another section of the sinking boat before the river engulfed it.

On the flats between them and the river they saw the dark smudge of waiting riders and two wagons, whose canvas canopies glowed palely. No one moved down there and Clay lifted an arm to halt his men as silently as possible. Those below heard nothing of the new arrivals because their ears were still ringing from the blast that had shattered the remains of the old riverboat.

A steam whistle hooted suddenly, bringing several startled whinnies from the Rectangle 5 mounts. A second strident shriek followed swiftly on the first and Clay's men saw the spurt of steam out on the dark river an instant before they heard the ear-piercing blast. It was close enough to the first siren call to cover the whinnying of their mounts.

But not entirely.

One of Donovan's rear riders fought his nervous horse as it spun around – he must have seen the bunched horsemen at the bottom of the slope. He yelled, then his gun was shooting holes in the sky.

'Mal! Mal! We're surrounded!'

Big Mal Donovan's booming voice roared: 'The hell. . . ?'

Donovan's words cut off as he hipped in saddle, saw Clay's men already spurring their mounts forward. He snatched his own six-gun and triggered two shots as his spur rowells raked viciously.

'Get them wagons outta here!' he thundered, but even as he shouted he saw there was nowhere to go, not only for the wagons but for his own men.

The creek was on one side, and Clay's men had spread out so that they cut off all retreat to the rear; that left only the river ahead. No way out there. They were trapped!

The large riverboat that was now arriving to pick up the shipment of guns was slowing, its huge stern paddlewheel whipping the Rio into foam and an insane cauldron of conflicting waves as it was desperately reversed.

Clay's riders were shooting now; their shots were answered in a wild volley by Donovan's band. Men on both sides were punched from their saddles. Horses reared, whinnying as lead found them. A man had his boot caught in the stirrup as his mount bolted and he was screaming as he bounced and slammed along until the back of his head pulped against a rock. But the horse kept going, wild-eyed, the corpse jarring along behind, leaving a gory trail.

Red leaned from the saddle as he rode up alongside a fleeing Broken D rider, jammed his already hot six-gun's muzzle under the rider's arm and blew him out of the saddle. Then an unseen slug punched into his body and he tilted wildly, lost his grip on the reins and fell under the hoofs of seven more horses charging through the mêlée.

Beef saw him go down, reined aside wildly as two Broken D riders converged on him. He slipped a leg over his saddle and, using an old Indian fighter's trick ducked under the straining neck. Holding by one hand, he shot both riders. One fell instantly under his mount's pounding hoofs. The other swayed, grabbed his chest, then yanked on the reins, pulling the galloping horse's head around too sharply. It lost stride, half-turned as its feet broke rhythm and they went down together, thrashing, spilling another rider who crashed into them.

Clay swerved to miss the pile-up, felt the hot air on his face as a bullet tore by. Instinctively he lurched his upper body forward on to the bay's arched neck. He twisted and saw a rider closing in, rifle at his shoulder. Clay's Colt bucked in his hand and suddenly the rider was airborne, arms and legs flailing before he struck the ground, sliding and somersaulting, his rifle skidding away.

The bay hauled up sharply, legs stiff, and Clay threw his full body weight against the straining reins. He was barely a yard from another horseman and there was no way to avoid a collision. He kicked his boots free of the stirrups and launched himself out of the saddle as the horses met with a meaty thud, interspersed with shrill whistles and snorts. He saw the other rider tumbling from leather, having made the same move as himself. Then the ground rushed up to meet him. Stars burst behind his eyes, his body was torn and wrenched, gravel ripped through his clothes, grazing his flesh.

He instinctively clenched his gun butt firmly as he rolled and bounced out of control. A pounding hoof slammed into the ground beside his head and for an instant he felt total panic at the thought of having his skull smashed like an eggshell. He covered his head with his arms and was still rolling with the impetus of his fall. Afterwards he figured out he must have rolled between the racing horse's front and back legs, and somehow had had enough speed to get through without being trampled. Talk about a cat having nine lives!

But for the moment all he knew was that he was choking on dust and grit and there was a red haze behind his eyes. He blinked violently, and his vision began to clear. He jumped to one side, dodged another horse and the boot the rider swung at his head.

In an apparently endless instant when all the action around him seemed to freeze, he recognized the rider: Big Mal Donovan. The man was already wrenching his mount around, half-leaning from the saddle, teeth bared, that one eye wide and wild. He had a Colt in each hand and he reared upright, thrusting both guns towards Clay Emory each time he pulled the triggers, stabbing them forward as if to drive his bullets home the harder into Clay's weaving body.

The left-hand gun blazed but only an empty chamber turned under the hammer of his right-hand weapon. Donovan's slug missed and Clay shoulder-rolled, came up on to one knee, left hand chopping at the hammer of his Colt.

It fired – once. Donovan lurched but roared a curse. Suddenly he was hurtling through the air. Clay tried to dodge but the massive weight bore him to the ground, crushed the breath from him, made his ribs creak. He fought back instinctively, hooking an elbow up under Donovan's jaw, catching him across the throat. The big rancher reared back, clawing at his throat, choking. Clay got out from under, sliding back on his shoulders.

As the battle raged around them, like the wartime Wilderness all over again, Big Mal came at him, huge hands clawed, ready to crush his neck, tear his head clear off his shoulders. Clay swung up his legs and drove both boots into the man's contorted face as he closed.

Donovan's head snapped back, his eyepatch wrenched off as his big body rolled awkwardly, legs working to keep balance. Beyond his clumsily moving body, Clay saw one of the racing wagons of guns shatter a wheel against a rock and the whole vehicle crashed on its side, catapulting the driver five yards.

The second wagon tried to dodge but the wreck was sliding right into the team of horses. As it shot into the air, discharging its load in a wild cascade of shattered boxes and weapons, Clay took a blow that almost caved in his chest.

Donovan had managed to get his feet under him. Clay spun on to hands and knees, scooped up a handful of gravel and threw it into the rancher's face.

Donovan roared like a mountain lion and lurched forward, unstoppable, like some vengeful giant in a kid's fairy tale. His eye patch was gone, revealing the empty socket, his big hands were opening and closing in their eagerness to feel Clay's body in their grip; his mouth was open, his teeth bared like a rampaging grizzly's.

Clay still held his empty Colt, reversed his grip and raised it like a club, changed his mind and flung it at Donovan's head. The big man dodged easily and grinned frighteningly as he lunged, long arms reaching out, grabbing one of Clay's shoulders. Clay groaned as he felt the bones crushing together under the strength of that grip. He thrashed wildly, yelling, and Donovan laughed.

He lifted Clay off the ground and shook him. Clay's teeth rattled, his eyes bulged. He kicked wildly and his boot took Big Mal just under the arch of the ribs. It didn't stop the man but it staggered him and as he gulped for air his grip loosened.

Clay wrenched free, fell, spun away as a boot heel drove at his face. He came up on hands and knees and scrabbled away like a spider as Donovan strode after him, wanting the thrill of crushing the life out of Clay between his own massive hands.

'Clay!'

He snapped his head around at the sound of his name. Dreamy, on his knees, blood trickling from a corner of his mouth, one hand clawing into his bleeding chest, swung his other hand and Clay caught the gleam of metal coming towards him. Later, he couldn't even remember reaching up almost in slow motion and plucking the spinning six-gun out of the air, then turning around on one leg, left hand slapping at the hammer spur in a blur of speed. His right forefinger depressed the trigger, the gun bucked and roared three times.

Donovan's huge frame shook as the bullets made a pattern on his great chest with no more spread than a playing card. He still kept coming, arms reaching for Clay as the gun hammer fell on an empty chamber.

Then, as his fingernails brushed Clay's throat he collapsed, as if every bone in his huge body had turned to jelly. One moment he was standing, ready to crush Emory, next he was a huddled heap at Clay's feet, his last breath rattling out of him.

Clay fell to his knees as the horsemen rode around him, chasing the gunrunners into the river or the creek; some were shouting that they were giving up. The riverboat's paddlewheel was churning wildly, the boat turning tightly. The bows just brushed a sandbank, but shuddered free and the vessel thrashed away back upriver, without its cargo of guns.

A few minutes later, the rattle of gunfire died.

*

Three Days Later. . . .

The Rectangle 5 looked like an army hospital with so many men sporting bandages or hobbling around on crude crutches and walking sticks.

Men who had not volunteered to go with Clay to stop the gunrunners were now cursing themselves. For the ones who had sided him, wounded or not, were sure enjoying their convalescence under Mattie's care and the food turned out by the soft-hearted cook.

The only sobering thought was that four men from the Five had died in the battle, Dreamy among them.

Clay Emory, with a new shirt now covering the bandages and plaster strips on his battered body, one strip showing above the right eye where a deep gash had been stitched by Beef, stood with his battered hat in his hand outside the ranch stables. The rested and contented bay stood by patiently as he spoke with Mattie.

'You surely turned this county upside down, Clay Emory,' she said, looking trim in her working jeans and checkered shirt, her hat resting on the back of her head, the henna hair catching the sun in a flaming glow.

Clay nodded, unable to keep his body-dragging weariness from showing. 'Gonna take me a week to write my report. The Chief calls it *The Battle of Manzano* and wants to take it to Washington and use it to back an appeal for more funds for the Patrol, while the Army's still clearing up along the river, and. . . .

159

Well, never mind that. We're still operational, that's what counts. I still have a job.'

Mattie sobered. 'That means . . . you'll move on?'

'There's always something to be done.'

'Where will you go?'

He shrugged. 'Wherever I'm told. It'll be some-where along the Texas–Mexico border, though, I guess.'

She seemed to brighten a little at that. 'Will you be coming back this way then? There'll always be a meal and a bed waiting for you.'

He stared soberly and saw the tension stiffen her body as he spoke.

'Mattie, there's not a hope in hell. . . .' he paused and smiled, 'that I won't come back this way!'

She stepped forward, clutched at one of his arms.

His other hand trembled a little as he lifted it ten-tatively and stroked that sun-warmed henna hair.

It felt good – *damned* good!